For fourteen years now *Perry Rhodan* has been acknowledged to be the world's top-selling science fiction series. Originally published in magazine form in Germany, the series has now appeared in hardback and paperback in the States.

Over five hundred *Perry Rhodan* clubs exist on the Continent and *Perry Rhodan* fan conventions are held annually. The first Perry Rhodan film, *SOS From Outer Space*, has now been released in Europe.

The series has sold over 140 million copies in Europe alone.

D1435112

Also available in the *Perry Rhodan* series

Kurt Mahr

PERRY RHODAN 17:

The Venus Trap

Futura Publications Limited
An Orbit Book

An Orbit Book

First published in Great Britain in 1976
by Futura Publications Limited
Copyright © 1972 by Ace Books
An Ace Book, by arrangement with
Arthur Moewig Verlag
Pursuit to Mars (aka '*Edison's Conquest of Mars*
& *Invasion of Mars*)
Revised Edition © 1969 by Forrest J Ackerman
A Martian Oddity (as *Behind the Ate Ball*)
Copyright © 1950 by Stadium Publishing Corp.
This series was created by Karl-Herbert Scheer and
Walter Ernsting, translated by Wendayne Ackerman
and edited by Forrest J Ackerman and Frederik Pohl

ISBN 0 8600 7902 3

This English edition is dedicated to the
Memory of Author RALPH MILNE FARLEY
and his Spaceman Myles Cabot Who had
Adventures on Venus even Before Perry.

Printed in Great Britain by
Richard Clay (The Chaucer Press), Ltd.,
Bungay, Suffolk
Futura Publications Limited,
110 Warner Road, Camberwell, London SE5

Chapter One

TROUBLE ON VENUS

LIFE—raw, primordial—teemed on the young world: on its land, beneath its seas and in its air. Prehistoric life forms, not dissimilar to those which once flourished on distant, early Earth—vicious, voracious but ... Venusian.

Venus, "the evening star," second from the sun, a hothouse of horrendous creatures: airborne, land-lubbing, oceanic.

Three Terranians found themselves on the surface of a Venusian sea: Perry Rhodan, John Marshall and Son Okura. Rhodan, the leader; Marshall, the esper, reader of minds; Okura the emfer, perceptor of electro-magnetic frequency wavelengths.

About the trio's boat the water gurgled sluggishly. It seemed to be thicker than on Earth, and so it was. A hand submerged in it emerged with a slimy coat for the water was so full of algae, single cells and other minute life forms that it acted like a collodial solution.

The boat plowed steadily through the impeding waves which were the last reminder of the terrible twilight storm that had swept over the flatland and the 200-mile-wide ocean channel more than eight hours before.

The sturdy little generator hummed monotonously, threatening to hypnotize heavy eyelids, lull weary men to sleep.

But to the coaxing arms of Morpheus they dared not submit—none of them! For more than a Terrestrial day they hadn't dared a wink. It had been difficult to stay awake in the darkness, especially for Perry with an unhealed wound paining his shoulder.

Perry Rhodan, President of the New Power, had come to Venus with the intention of restoring order once again but, due to a chain of calamitous circumstances, had been cast with two companions almost helplessly into the wilderness.

At the present time he was far from achieving his goal. There were still 180 miles of water to be crossed in the boat, 180 miles of unknown dangers and 180 miles wherein at any time Col. Raskujan's helicopters could swoop down and attack the defenseless little lifeboat. Darkness per se afforded no guarantee of protection from the colonel's fightercraft for the aerial attackers were equipped with the latest infrared searchlights.

"I wonder if they've noticed yet that we swiped their boat," John Marshall wondered aloud.

Nobody knew. They'd surreptitiously taken possession of the boat from one of Raskujan's helicopters at the height of the battle between the colonel's and Tomisenkov's troops.

"I guess sooner or later they'll discover the loss of the boat," Perry replied.

"And then?" It was Son Okura, the Japanese, who spoke.

Rhodan shrugged his shoulders—and immediately regretted it: the sudden movement made his injury ache. "Raskujan will rack his brains over it. Right now we don't know whether he's even aware of our existence."

"Tomisenkov will be eager to tell him all about us," Marshall commented.

But Rhodan wasn't at all convinced. "You're misjudging Tomisenkov," he explained. "I've heard the radio conversation between him and Raskujan. The colonel has the men of his reinforcement fleet well in hand. Simply because his men have been well fed, there've been no mutineering tendencies. Tomisenkov's troops, on the other hand, are disorganized. Now Tomisenkov demands that Raskujan submit to him as a general, while Raskujan as a colonel insists that Tomisenkov has lost all rights commensurate with his rank due to his rebellion and the deterioration of his troops. They're both members of the Eastern Bloc but fierce rivals. I don't believe Tomisenkov is willing to give any information to Raskujan. The experience Tomisenkov gained on Venus is very valuable to Raskujan. This knowledge probably gives him a measure of reassurance and he can afford to keep his mouth shut."

Okura was about to reply something when Marshall called with a muffled voice from the bow: "Stop the boat!"

Rhodan reacted instantaneously. He pushed the lever to lift the little propeller out of the water. The hum of the idling motor slid a few notes up the scale before Rhodan switched it off.

Everything was quiet around them—except for the splashing of the languid waves.

"What's the matter?" Rhodan asked.

"There!" Marshall answered, pointing with his hand.

Rhodan moved forward and looked. He had no trouble seeing the fluorescent shimmer on the water at a distance of about three hundred feet and spreading out as far as the eye could see to the east and west.

Rhodan became apprehensive.

"What is it?" Marshall asked perplexed. "It can't be a ..."

Rhodan nodded. "Yes. It's a jellyfish. The biggest one I've ever seen."

Son Okura also came to the bow. He was capable of receiving certain wavelengths in the electro-magnetic frequency band which were beyond the perception of normal eyes. Thus he saw infra-red heat waves and ultra-violet radiation as distinctly as visible light.

"What can you see?" Rhodan asked.

Okura narrowed his eyes. The warm water of the Venusian ocean was for him like a carpet flooded with light. The jellyfish, however, which absorbed a part of the water's heat and reflected another portion into the ocean, appeared on his retina as a long dark stretch.

"It extends about two miles to the west," Okura said, "and as far east as I can see."

Rhodan considered. "Alright, then we'll go west to get around it." He started the motor up again and immersed the propeller in the water. Swinging the rudder hard to starboard, he steered the boat around in a sharp curve.

"Is it that dangerous?" Marshall wanted to know.

"Have you ever seen one of these jellyfish?"

"No. Only a small one in a bay."

Rhodan gave an understanding smile. "I'll give you a demonstration. In any case, we'd have been lost if we'd run into it. There's more power in this thin carpet of jellyfish than in 10 motors like ours."

The boat proceeded now on a northwesterly course. Rhodan tried to follow around the western rim as closely as possible. The boat had a speed of about 20 miles an hour. They could ill afford to lose even a precious second on a detour.

About ten minutes later they were due west of the jellyfish carpet. John Marshall was fascinated by the sight. The flourescence was composed of many different blending colors and presented a spectacle of beauty in motion that never failed to impress Rhodan, too, no matter how often he had seen it before.

It was hard to believe that this carpet of light was in reality a single animal spread out flat on the water and lurking for prey. The beauty was a deceptive mask for the enormous voracity and irresistible power exercised by the jellyfish to drag its victims to the depths.

Rhodan took a few heavy steel nuts out of the boat's toolbox and stood beside Marshall. The western side of the jellyfish was no more than 50 feet away from the wall of the boat.

"Okura!" Rhodan said softly.

"Yes, sir!"

"Are you ready to close the boat covers? Wait for my signal."

The Japanese nodded. Rhodan handed the nuts to Marshall.

"Toss them in!"

Marshall weighed the heavy metal pieces carefully in his hand. Then he swung his arm back and pitched them all together far onto the colorful and shimmering jellyfish.

The reaction was instantaneous. The nuts had hardly touched the animal when the colors began to fade away. Within a few seconds the glittering ceased completely. A rumbling noise started as the gigantic jellyfish began to contract itself around the spot where it had been hit by the nuts in order to pull down its catch.

The first breakers hit the boat. About 100 feet from the boat, the heretofore peaceful fluorescing carpet had formed a hemispheric lump of nondescript color.

The waves threw up foamy crests as the huge mass of jellyfish commenced to submerge. Marshall gaped with open mouth and wide eyes and lost his hold as the boat began to roll. He'd have gone overboard if Rhodan hadn't grabbed him just in time.

"Watch out!" Rhodan shouted.

Son Okura held his hand on the inclosure.

The jellyfish was still growing. Now shaped like a sphere, the lower part of its gelatinous body was sinking with ever increasing speed deeper into the water. A few moments before the creature's body had been spread out over a few square miles of the ocean's surface; now, in a matter of seconds, it contracted into a compact volume, creating in its proximity heavy storm-sized swells.

Rhodan let Marshall watch the strange display until

the boat had taken on so much water that it was a serious hazard. Only then did he shout to Okura: "Close up and hang on!"

Okura pulled the flexible cover up, securing the boat against the huge waves threatening to sink it. Marshall went down flat on the bottom of the boat and held onto the safety straps at the walls. After closing the cover the Japanese was thrown from his feet by a tremendous breaker and hurtled across Marshall.

For the next 10 minutes the ocean played ball with them. The boat spun around its axis. A severe jolt strained Rhodan's wound and forced him to release his grip on the safety strap. Son Okura, who was unable to grab a hold in time, was turned upside down and rolled against the toolbox in the bow with an audible crash.

After several fruitless attempts Rhodan managed to work his way to the motor and shut it off. The constantly changing load was hard on the motor and it was useless in the violent disturbance anyhow.

Marshall, for whom the show had been performed, lay in the middle of the boat swearing loudly. He was still swearing when the sea finally calmed down and Rhodan told the Japanese to open the boat.

Marshall pulled himself up to the rim of the boat. "I didn't think it could be that bad," he panted.

Rhodan smiled ruefully. "Next time you'll know better. There's nothing more treacherous than a Venusian jellyfish." He started the motor up again and set his course. He had no idea how far the boat had been driven off its course by the incident but he didn't figure that it could have been enough to make a substantial difference for the landing on the northern continent.

For awhile they were kept busy scooping out the water with which they were inundated by the waves the monstrous jellyfish had stirred up. Although the work was easy they became quite exhausted. They sat leaning against the wall of their boat for some time fighting the fatigue that threatened to close their eyes.

If it hadn't been for the ambitious aspirations of the Eastern Bloc's government, Rhodan wouldn't have been exposed to such a precarious situation as that in which he now found himself. That government was overthrown a year ago after it had taken advantage of Rhodan's absence to launch two great spacefleets destined for Venus for the purpose of wresting the base of the New Power from them. Without their brazen interference, Rhodan thought, he'd probably be somewhere else, safe and sound.

Rhodan would have kept philosophizing to himself but Okura suddenly jumped up in the bow of the boat with an astonished cry.

Rhodan saw that he stared into the sky. He followed with his eyes but was unable to detect anything. "What's the matter, Son?" he called. "What do you see?"

As Rhodan went close to him, he could see that Okura's eyes were wide open in anguish. He breathed heavily and before he could answer, Rhodan heard the swishing noise that came from above and filled him for a second with the same fright as the Japanese.

"A flying reptile!" Okura gasped. "About northeast but flying straight toward us."

"How high?"

"Approximately 300 feet."

"Big?"

The Japanese wrinkled his brow. "A wingspan of 100 feet, I'd say."

They waited. The droning that brought the tension of their nerves nearly to the breaking point came closer and grew louder.

"It'll soon be on top of us," the Japanese murmured. And then: "It's turning now and circling above us!"

Rhodan's shoulders drooped. "Son, you stay at the bow. Marshall, take the center. I'll go to the motor. From now on we'll have to remain still. Son will tell us when the beast swerves down. If it does, we must fire at it. Take careful aim so we won't have to shoot more than once. The thermo-beams will be visible for several hundred miles. I don't have to explain to you what will happen if Raskujan's observers notice our shots."

Several minutes passed. The motor hummed monotonously and the sluggish water splashed softly.

A shrill scream from Okura broke the ominous quiet:

"Here it comes!"

Colonel Raskujan's relief armada landed at the same place as General Tominsekov had touched down earlier with his 500 spaceships.

Raskujan turned out to be a great deal luckier than the general. Tomisenkov's first encampment had been blown to smithereens and cast to the winds by the

13

tornado created in the wake of the *Stardust*. Tomisenkov's undamaged ships were hidden in the mountains where they were put out of action one by one in systematic pursuit by Rhodan.

Thus Raskujan had found an unobstructed field for his landing. The *Stardust* had scorched a wide strip straight through the jungle as it flew across Tomisenkov's camp, leaving it with blackened and glazed earth. Raskujan had started out from Terra with 200 ships. At that time he still served under Major General Pjotkin. Thirty-four of those ships were lost when the *Stardust*, on its way back to Earth from Venus, slammed through the fleet and incinerated in its formidable defense screen the helpless vehicles from the Eastern Bloc. Among them was the flagship with Major General Pjotkin on board.

Raskujan reassembled the vessels which had escaped the holocaust and continued to Venus. Another 43 ships were destroyed in the aerodynamic landing maneuver. They crashed and sank as fiery bright meteors in the oceans and forests of Venus.

A total of 123 ships had withstood the flight intact and landed proudly on Tomisenkov's original airfield. Their mobility, however, was severely restricted by a lack of fuel.

No trace of Tomisenkov could be found at that time. Colonel Raskujan assumed responsibility and he had to use his own judgment as to the best way of achieving success for the enterprise.

This didn't appear to him to be very difficult. His superiors were interested in gaining control of the New Power's fortress. Since Rhodan was absent from Venus at the time of the arrival of his reinforcement fleet, Raskujan believed that the base was unguarded and considered its conquest child's play.

Raskujan had to revise his ideas about "fortifications." For almost a year he daily butted his head against a wall. Rhodan had surrounded the bulwark with an impenetrable protective screen. Among the members of Raskujan's expedition were many scientists and technicians. These experts were—for reasons unknown to Raskujan—mostly women. But even the most skillful technicians were stymied by the forbidding energy screen.

When Raskujan had reached a dead end, his attention was diverted. The first trace of General Tomisenkov and his men was found on a peninsula which extended south from the big northern continental landmass. It was engulfed by a sea channel of the great primordial ocean.

Raskujan, whose orders had been to bring relief and support to Tominsenkov's troops, began to collect information. He learned that Tomisenkov's Space Landing Division had become disorganized under the terrible conditions of life on Venus and suffered serious mutiny.

Subsequently Raskujan had mapped his plans. Tomisenkov and his men had to be subjugated.

As Raskujan had the necessary means to carry out his plans against Tomisenkov's disillusioned soldiers, he succeeded in taking the general himself prisoner as well as many of his followers. Furthermore, he was able to seize Thora, the Arkonide woman, who became his most important captive. Thora had been the greatest source of the knowledge which enabled Rhodan to establish the New Power.

Raskujan was triumphant—until he realized that Thora had as much respect for him as for one of the pesky Venusian flies.

She refused to answer any of his questions, let alone advise him how to enter the fortress through the energy curtain.

Then he turned to Tomisenkov. But this prisoner didn't treat him much better than Thora, which dismayed him even more. Raskujan's character was basically that of a subordinate afflicted with an inferiority complex. Since he screwed up his courage to attack a general and capture him, he expected him to behave as a prisoner—not as a general.

Since he had been defeated and brought in with one of Raskujan's helicopters, Tomisenkov had already had to undergo five interrogations. For a man who had steeled his nerves for a year against the dangers of the Venusian jungle, they represented only harmless quizzes, especially as Raskujan's intelligence officers seemed to suffer from the same inferiority complex as their superior when confronted with a general, even though he was stripped of his insignia.

When the storm had calmed down after dusk, Raskujan summoned the prisoner to the command center of his flagship.

Raskujan received him with a submachinegun displayed ostentatiously across his knees. He didn't even offer a seat to Tomisenkov.

"I understand that you refuse to cooperate with my command," Raskujan began.

Tomisenkov didn't seem to consider this opening as a question; at any rate, he gave no answer.

"Answer me!" Raskujan bellowed angrily.

"Answer what?" Tomisenkov said calmly.

"Why you don't cooperate with me!"

Tomisenkov grinned wryly. "Why don't you cooperate with *me?*" he countered with the same question.

Raskujan gasped for breath. Then he made the mistake of giving explanations in reply to Tomisenkov's question. "Because your division is wracked by dissension and rebellion."

"That doesn't make it right. You've been sent here to bring me support—and to give me moral support if that is necessary. That was indeed the case. However, instead of making an effort to locate my division and to help reorganize it, you chose to remain here and to make dozens of crazy attempts to get into Rhodan's base. And when you finally found out where I was, you had nothing better to do than to assault us! Us, to whom you were supposed to bring help!"

Raskujan barely managed to keep his composure. "As a former officer you know as well as I do how demoralizing your men would have been for my troops. I had no other choice than to draw a line between us. My regiment has nothing in common any more than your division."

Tomisenkov made such a derisive gesture that Raskujan was hard put to control his anger.

"Don't try to outsmart me," Tomisenkov interjected. "You forget that you were serving in my company. I've known you for years. Even as a young lieutenant you tried to show off whenever you had a chance. No, Raskujan, you can't get away with it as easy as that. You thought that you had the opportunity here on Venus to play the big chief. The only one who could have spoiled it for you was I, who outrank you. That's why you pulled a fast one and tried to eliminate me."

Raskujan had jumped up. It took a long time before he found his tongue again. "That's ... that's ... you're forgetting that you're my ..."

At this point the buzzing of a radio set interrupted Raskujan's stammering. He turned around and hit the button of the receiver with the palm of his hand.

"An unusual flash of light has been observed, sir," the monitor reported quickly. "Direction 180 degrees, distance approximately 150 miles."

Raskujan raised his eyebrows. "Describe it to me!" he demanded.

"It resembled a cone of light from three searchlights, sir," the observer answered. "However the intensity of the light exceeded ordinary searchlights."

"How many times did you notice this effect?"

"Only once, sir!"

"Alright!"

The report was ended. Raskujan made another connection. A raspy voice answered.

"Take two of your helicopters, Captain," Raskujan ordered, "and search the ocean. Determine the direction where the strange light came from through the observation post. I want to know what it is."

The captain affirmed the order. Raskujan switched off the transmitter and turned back to Tomisenkov.

Tomisenkov smiled.

"What's there to grin about?" Raskujan asked gruffly.

"I think," Tomisenkov said softly, savoring the effect his words had on Raskujan, "there's somebody on your heels who will teach a shabby colonel how to behave on Venus."

The swishing noise rose to a roar as the flying reptile swooped down. Rhodan stood slanted against the edge of the boat and stared in the direction of the sound. He saw only a giant shadow which passed with incredible speed over the boat and disappeared again in the dark.

The sound became more distant and weaker. It remained for a few seconds at the same level, then swelled up again.

Rhodan wondered how much of a risk he could take. It was impossible to know on which one of its passes the winged lizard would attack. Perhaps it wouldn't. But it would be too late to shoot at it if it had one of the three in its claws.

The droning grew louder.

"Fire when it flies over us," Rhodan called decisively.

They raised the barrels of their weapons in the direction of the predator. The menacing noise kept growing until their ears droned.

And then It appeared again.

A black shadow in the gray darkness, larger than before but of ill-defined shape.

Rhodan followed the shadow with the barrel of his

impulse-beamer and as the lizard hovered above the boat he ordered: "Fire!"

Brilliant white-blue flashes of concentrated heat rays shot from the funnel-shaped muzzles of the barrels, illuminating for a fraction of a second the horrible body of the aerial lizard covered with a leathery skin and consuming it with its full power.

The savage scream uttered by the beast must have been audible for miles around. But it didn't last long. A few hundred thousand megawatts of thermal energy killed the reptile and it fell burning into the ocean.

Rhodan dropped his weapon and grabbed the rudder. He cut straight through the huge frontal wave thrown up by the impact of the behemoth, then pushed the rudder hard to the side and steered in a wide curve to the east.

After 20 minutes Rhodan put the boat on the original course again. Moving the rudder around, done by habit with his right arm, caused the injury in his shoulder to hurt again. He cursed his helplessness and wished he had his Arkonide medicaments on hand. It would have taken no more than a few hours to put him back in shape.

Son Okura still sat at the bow scanning northward. Only Marshall seemed to assume that the worst danger had been overcome by the extermination of the flying lizard. He was lying in the center of the boat with his arms folded under his head.

"Don't be lazy, man. Better get up!" Rhodan said. "We'll soon be real busy."

Marshall was frightened. "What's up now?" he asked gloomily.

"The light effects are inseparable from the heat emission of thermal weapons and they can be seen for 300 miles in clear weather," Rhodan pointed out. "You can figure out what that means."

Marshall got up with a sigh. "Well," he murmured, "and what can we do if your expectations materialize?"

Rhodan grinned. "Keep shooting," he answered dryly.

The captain dispatched by Raskujan with two helicopters had little trouble locating the lifeboat which was quite conspicuous.

From a distance of 50 miles he detected a weak but unmistakable blip on the radar screen and from 300 feet he clearly recognized the boat with the infra-red searchlight and saw the three man crew through the night binoculars.

The captain warned his gunner to be cautious and gave the same instructions to the second helicopter.

Then he descended and prudently approached the boat.

They could hear the whirring of the rotor blades and the high whistling of the engine jets. Son Okura saw two machines coming at considerable height from the north.

They were no surprise for Rhodan. He had expected them.

Okura suddenly flinched back from his observation post in the bow of the boat and threw his arms over his face with a startled scream. It was at the moment when the captain shined his infra-red searchlight on the boat and saw it through the filter.

Rhodan tried to outguess his antagonists.

He'll recognize the boat, he figured. *He also knows that Raskujan has lost none of his helicopters. Therefore, he'll take us for Tomisenkov's men or—*

Before he could come to a conclusion, the two crafts had arrived and the speed with which they were coming in left no doubt about their intention of attacking the boat.

"Down flat on the bottom of the boat!" Rhodan shouted. "Keep your guns up!"

Marshall and Okura complied at once. An automatic cannon began to chatter and a second one joined in. Rhodan could feel the boat jerk and he heard above the din how the motor changed its sound. Then he saw the shadow of the first helicopter on top of them.

He didn't know whether Okura or Marshall had already fired as he saw no flashes from their weapons. He braced the butt of his thermo-beamer against his chest so that the barrel pointed straight up and pulled the trigger.

The discharge was completely free of recoil. As if fired from a toy, the brightly flashing beam shot up in the dark and caught the helicopter before it peeled off to the side. There was a thunderous detonation as its fuel exploded and a rain of luminous metal parts fell hissing into the water around their boat.

The second machine observed how the first one was brought down and turned away in time. Far out it continued flying in low circles around the boat.

Rhodan kept low and crawled forward in the boat.

Marshall was lying as he had been ordered. He grinned when he saw Rhodan.

Son Okura got up on his knees and watched the second aircraft flying around the boat. Rhodan switched on his wristband transceiver and scanned the frequency range of the receiver. He could hear nothing except the static of the atmosphere. The helicopter pilot had so far not considered it necessary to inform his base about the incident.

Rhodan was certain that he either would report the skirmish or attempt a second attack.

They waited for the next sortie.

Okura raised his right arm. "The circles are getting tighter," he called.

Rhodan looked over the rim of the boat but couldn't see a thing. "How close is it now?" he asked.

"Average distance about 500 feet," the Japanese answered.

Rhodan reflected. "Let's show them what we think of them!" he called to Okura.

They're making a mistake, Rhodan thought. *They want to try out how far we can shoot with our rayguns. They don't know that an impulse-beamer works with maximum energy to the limit of its range. They think they can wait till we fire the first shot and still scram in time!*

Okura kneeled behind the wall and supported his raygun on the rim. He pressed his eyes together and tilted his head forward when the infra-red beam of the vehicle swept over him.

Then he took careful aim. Rhodan saw his fingers curl around the trigger but was startled nonetheless

23

when the finger-sized blue-white beam flashed from the muzzle.

Raskujan's helicopter didn't have a chance. It dropped into the ocean and exploded, hissing violently.

Rhodan breathed a sigh of relief. He went past Marshall to the motor. In his haste he had only been able to tie up the rudder loosely and now—

He was taken aback when he reached the stern. He saw a frazzled piece of the strap he had used to fasten the rudder lying on the bottom. No sign of the rudder could be found.

He went down to examine the motorblock encased in a light metal box. He discovered the trace of a shell and the spot where it had exploded. It had torn off the rudder and demolished the motor.

Rhodan banged against the metal housing with his fists. Previously it could only be removed with screwdrivers and boltcutters. Now he shook it loose with a few knocks and was soon easily able to pull it down with his hands.

He saw at a glance what had happened. The shell had exploded near the small efficient turbine. The turbine was no longer recognizable, just a formless lump of metal blackened by powder.

Rhodan got up. He felt weak in the knees but soon regained his strength.

"The boat is intact," Marshall announced happily. "All bullet holes have probably sealed themselves. We haven't taken on any appreciable quantity of water."

Rhodan's face was set. He walked stiffly through the swaying boat toward Marshall. Marshall noticed how serious he looked. "What . . . ?"

Rhodan put his hand on his shoulder and said quietly: "Start making your calls again, Marshall. Our motor is destroyed and we can't repair it. I figure we're about 130 miles from the coast of the northern continent and about 80 miles from the southern shore. We can move neither forward nor back. Try once more to get in touch with the seals."

And with a cheerless smile he added: "Otherwise we'll have to swim."

Chapter Two

S.O.S.! "SAVE US, SEALS!"

Raskujan had argued with Tomisenkov for almost an hour, forgetting that it was quite unnecessary for him to have discussions with a prisoner. But then came the report that two more of the unusual bursts of light had been observed over the open sea. As he hadn't heard from the helicopters since he sent them out on their mission, he began to worry about them and had Tomisenkov taken away by the two guards before he witnessed the failure of the task force and gloated over it.

Tomisenkov walked willingly between the two guards across the landing site devoid of any vegetation. The two guards delivered him to four other guards posted at the gate, who took him to his own tent where a personal guard took over.

Tomisenkov studied the layout of the prison camp for very good reasons. He memorized daily without a map what his trained eyes had seen. He could have found his way with closed eyes. Thus the pitch dark night of Venus was the best time for his scheme because Raskujan's soldiers would stumble blindly around in the dark to which they were not yet accustomed.

He laid his plans calmly and methodically. His tent had no floor cover. The soil of the ground had been solidly compacted. Tomisenkov took off one of his boots and began to scrape the ground and fill the boot with the removed soil.

After a few minutes the boot was full and Tomisenkov packed it in tightly to the top. He weighed his odd tool in his right hand. It had the similar feel and weight of a sack of sand.

Then he looked around in his tent. It was fairly small and well-lit. Tomisenkov picked out a corner best suited for his purpose.

Unfortunately, he couldn't do much about the electric bulb illuminating his tent. Of course, he could have broken it, but then—

He squatted in the rear corner of the tent with his back toward the entrance and stared ostensibly at the ground. Now that everything had been prepared, he started to yell.

"Guard! Guaaaaard!"

He sounded terrified and the result was immediately apparent. The entrance to the tent was flung open. Tomisenkov turned his face around and tried to look frightened.

"What's going on?" the guard shouted.

Tomisenkov was breathless and made a few gestures with his hands. "Here ..." he panted, "in the corner ... quick!"

There was a great variety of monsters on Venus, among them those that could bore their way through the ground and pop up unexpectedly in the middle of a tent. The guard was aware of the peril. He entered with his gun drawn and motioned Tomisenkov to the side as he approached the corner.

Tomisenkov made way for him. "Sort of a worm ...!" he groaned. He positioned himself so that he cast his shadow into the corner the sentry examined. When the man had passed him he picked up the boot filled with dirt.

"Get out of the light!" the guard ordered and waved his hand without looking back.

Tomisenkov got out of the light—a step behind the back of the guard. He made sure that the guard was unable to see his shadow. Then he raised the heavy boot and whacked the guard over the head. The man toppled forward to the ground.

Tomisenkov proceeded to empty the soil from his boot and stamp it back into the ground with his foot. Then he took out the rope he'd fashioned from the tent's fabric and tied the unconscious man up. He also stuffed his handkerchief into his mouth and fastened it so that the victim couldn't push the gag out with his tongue.

Finally he shoved the sentry behind his cot to keep him out of sight of a casual glance from the entrance. He placed the gun on the bed where the guard could see it when he woke up.

Then he left his tent.

He had no trouble getting to the largest of the tents 300 feet away—even though sentries tried to look as if nothing could escape them.

Actually they're scared, Tomisenkov thought contemptuously. *They're afraid that giant white worms or voracious scaly vermin will crawl out of the ground and drag them away.*

They even whistled some tunes to hide their fears.

It took Tomisenkov 15 minutes to cover the distance of 300 feet.

When Tomisenkov reached the tent he saw that three guards were posted at the entrance. However, this was no problem. The walls of the tent didn't touch the ground except where they were fastened with ropes to the stakes. In between there was room enough for a man to squeeze through by lifting up the side.

Tomisenkov crawled in under the wall. A light was burning inside.

He heard a soft cry of surprise. He slipped inside and got up. He quickly put his index finger to his lips and made a warning gesture toward the entrance.

Then he took time out to greet Thora, the woman from Arkon, with a silent bow.

Thora's home was far distant from Terra and its solar system. Much farther than Tomisenkov could imagine in spite of his excellent education.

Thora, who was shipwrecked on the Moon in her exploration cruiser 10 years earlier, had begun to co-operate with Perry Rhodan, helping him to create the stable framework of the unprecedented New Power.

Until a few days ago, Thora had been Tomisenkov's prisoner.

"Regardless what you may think of me," Tomisenkov said hastily, "please, don't make a noise! I'm not going to harm you."

Thora gave no answer. She twisted her lips slightly and displayed a smile so derisive and ironic that Tomisenkov had trouble controlling his anger.

"I don't have much time," he continued. "The

guards are inspected every 50 minutes. I'll have to leave here in 15 minutes at the latest."

Thora's scornful look irritated him.

He endeavored to formulate his offer precisely. "I'd like to work together with you," he began.

Thora didn't deem his proposition worthy of an answer.

"As you know," Tomisenkov went on, "it wouldn't be difficult at all to overpower Raskujan's guards. Our troubles would begin when we leave the camp. We'll have no weapons other than those we take away from the guards. Raskujan has helicopters and a lot of other equipment. He could catch us an hour after we made our escape. For this reason, we'd have to know where to go when we break out. It would be up to you to give us the right information."

Thora stared at him with unrelenting contempt. "And you think that I'd fall for such a clumsy trick!" she finally replied.

"No trick! Think about it. What reason could I have to deceive you? The simple fact is, we're both in the same boat. It doesn't serve any useful purpose to sit in the camp with our hands folded in our laps while we wait for a miracle to happen."

Thora appeared to mull over his words. "And what guarantee do I have that your designs won't get me —to use one of your phrases—from the frying pan into the fire?" she asked skeptically.

Tomisenkov shrugged his shoulders. "If you can't see the difference between my goals and Raskujan's ambitions, you don't know people," he replied dejectedly.

Thora laughed mockingly. "All I know is that people have the urge to bash in each other's heads."

Tomisenkov got up. "Yes, of course," he muttered angrily. "Your race has never done anything like that. You were all born innocent babes and remained so forever." He gave Thora no chance to answer him. "I've offered you my cooperation," he declared. "At this point I think you'd benefit more from our collaboration than I. I'll stick to my offer. Think about it. I'll drop in again a little later to hear your decision. Goodby!"

He bent down and crawled out under the wall of the tent.

Fifteen minutes later he returned to his own tent without having encountered any untoward incidents. The guard he had overwhelmed was conscious again and stared at him with wild eyes. Tomisenkov squatted down before him and said, "Listen to me, my boy. You can see that I've left your gun lying here. I took a little walk which you'd not have permitted me to do if I'd asked you. So I was forced to keep you out of my way for a little while and I'm sorry if I hurt you. In a few minutes there'll be the inspection of the guards. By that time you'll be free, your gun strapped on again. All I care about now is whether you're going to report this little affair or prefer to keep quiet about it. You can imagine that I won't tell them anything myself."

With these words he began to untie the soldier. He removed the gag last. "Get up, my boy," he told him.

The guard was dumbfounded and awkwardly arose.

His first move was to reach for his gun. Then he stared suspiciously at Tomisenkov.

Tomisenkov returned his gaze without blinking. After awhile he asked: "Did I give you a headache?"

This seemed to surprise the soldier. He shook his head. Then they both started to laugh. Tomisenkov gave him a friendly slap on the shoulder. "You're alright, Corporal," he said. "I'll remember you when this unpleasantness is behind us."

The guard left the tent and began to ponder what Tomisenkov could have meant. He was so busy thinking about it that he let the inspection pass and only said:

"Corporal Wlassow! All is well."

For two hours John Marshall had continuously kept sending out his calls with his remarkable telepathic power. "Come help us, seals! We're friends in distress!"

Two hours he waited, hoping that the shiny head of a seal would bob up from the water near the immobilized boat, but he waited in vain. Nothing showed up and the uninterrupted strain created a world of dancing colorful rings before his eyes.

The luring telepathic calls had drained his body of its last strength. He knew that the seals were not living in the ocean. They inhabited the environment of the coast, preferably sea inlets cutting deep into the mountains like fjords. The closest shore was at least 60 miles from the present position of their boat.

Marshall had tried very hard to bridge this distance but he could feel his head swimming and realized that he'd be unable to keep it up much longer.

A few more minutes, maybe eight or ten. That would be the end.

Son Okura crouched apathetically at the forward end. From time to time he raised his head and scanned the ocean. Nothing. No menace and nothing to interrupt the monotony of waiting in the night.

Perry Rhodan spent his time listening and mediating. He weighed alternative solutions to their present situation in case Marshall's calls were without success. Rhodan knew very little about the seals. It had been determined that they possessed a certain degree of intelligence—enough to have a language of their own —and that they should thus to able to respond to a telepathic message. What he didn't know was how they would react to such a message, assuming they received it. Perhaps it was a matter of indifference to the seals that they drifted helplessly out in the open sea.

His listening was concentrated on some noise he expected to hear within the next hour. Considerable time had elapsed since they shot down the helicopters. Irrespective of what one might think of Colonel Raskujan's military prowess, sooner or later he was bound to dispatch a squadron of helicopters to check on the fate of the first two machines.

In that case it would be the sheerest luck if their floundering life raft escaped their notice.

Nobody can depend on such luck when making plans, Rhodan mused philosophically. Son Okura's muffled call aroused him. "They're coming!"

Rhodan jumped to his feet. "Who's coming?"

Okura too had leaped up and leaned far out over the rounded bow of the boat. Rhodan noticed that he looked at the surface of the water, not at the sky.

The Japanese stretched his arm out. "There ... the seals!"

Rhodan heard a slight splashing which didn't coincide with the rhythm of the ground swell. Something dark and shiny emerged a few feet from the boat and approached hesitantly.

"Marshall, come here!" Rhodan called.

Marshall pushed himself up from the side of the boat and staggered forward. Meanwhile the heads of other seals surfaced and came closer. Rhodan counted a total of 30.

It was obvious that Marshall was unable to stand it much longer. Rhodan patted him gently on the shoulder and said: "Only a few more moments, then it'll be over and done with. Explain our situation to them!"

Marshall leaned over the bow to get as close as possible to the seals and to support his tired body. He described in simple, easily comprehensible thoughts what had happened to them and the kind of help they needed.

Fortunately, the seals were not slow to understand and, most of all, they were eager to be helpful. Marshall advised Rhodan of their suggestion. "They can pull our boat if we've got enough ropes. They want to form teams of ten and take turns on the way."

Rhodan agreed. "That's about the way I imagined it. O.K., we've got the ropes."

They cut up the long anchor line in suitable pieces,

used the landing ropes to make slings and tied them together, following the instructions by the seals as transmitted by Marshall. The entire task took less than 15 minutes. The seals slipped into the slings before they could sink and pulled them tight with their strong flippers. The thin ropes didn't hurt their leathery skin over the layers of fat.

"The seals are asking where we want to go," Marshall inquired.

Rhodan thought for a moment. "Ask them if they can take us to the peninsula where it joins the coast of the continent."

"Nothing to it," Marshall reported their answer.

Rhodan wanted to say something but the boat surged forward at the same instant. The seals required no further instructions. With a speed exceeding that of their old motor by more than half—as Rhodan estimated—their unwieldy craft streaked through the waves.

Marshall was lost in thought as he gazed on the glistening heads of the seals pulling the boat and those swimming along to their left and right.

Then he flopped down on the bottom of the boat. The back of his head landed in a puddle of slimy water they had failed to scoop out. This didn't bother him though. He had hardly laid down when he was fast asleep.

Rhodan and the Japanese exchanged understanding glances. They both crouched at the bow of the boat and watched the seals. Rhodan found it amazing that 10 seals imparted a higher velocity to the boat than the 30 horsepower turbine. One and a half times the velocity meant more than twice the output, assuming the efficiency was equal. Under these conditions it could be figured that each of the 10 seals developed about 10 horsepowers.

Their efficiency was probably higher than that of the more complicated motor with its propeller drive. But a minimum of at least four or five horsepower had to be ascribed to the seals.

For the first time Rhodan understood how different life on this young world was from ancient Terra. For the first time he grasped the meaning of the concept of vitality.

Colonel Raskujan committed the error of worrying more about his two most important prisoners, Thora and Tomisenkov, than about the two gyrocopters he had sent out.

He requested information about the aircraft from the radio station which had been set up some distance away from the spaceships in the vicinity of the coast and learned that nothing had been heard from them for two hours. The period of two hours didn't disturb him as such. A search over the open sea could easily require three or four times as long without producing any results but the radio silence caused him anxiety.

The radio station had attempted several times to contact the two machines, each time without success.

Now Raskujan decided quickly. He gave orders to a major to comb the surface of the ocean with three helicopter squadrons—giving special attention to the area where the strange streams of light had been observed. They were to look for the missing vehicles and spot any enemies who were around, to attack and destroy the enemy or capture him if possible.

The helicopters took off within a few minutes after Raskujan issued his command. But meanwhile three hours had elapsed since they had last heard from the first two vehicles.

Two hours had gone by since the seals had taken over leading the boat. Rhodan estimated they had covered a distance of about 50 miles during these two hours. As the boat was proceeding now in a north-northeast direction, the distance to their hypothetical point of landing had grown by a few more miles. Rhodan guessed that they were about 90 miles from their goal, a ride of nearly four hours.

He wondered what steps Raskujan had taken about his two machines that had disappeared. He didn't trust his luck to be great enough to make Raskujan refrain from any further action. Sooner or later more helicopters probing the ocean were bound to come forth.

The only chance their little boat had against a flotilla of helicopters—except for their thermo-beam weapons—lay in the fact that they had put a considerable distance between themselves and the course on which the helicopters would presumably fly from their camp. Perhaps the search would take long enough to permit the safe escape of their boat.

Perhaps—

Rhodan was still mulling over these thoughts when a sound reached his ears that was different from the splashing noise of the seals. He tried to shield his ears from the splashing of the water with his hands and listened into the night.

Irregular, humming sounds.

Helicopters! An entire squadron!

Still far away, Rhodan thought. *Okura won't be able to see them yet.*

Nevertheless, he drew the attention of the Japanese to the noise and told him to keep his eyes open. As Okura could not have failed to see the hot exhaust from the engine jets if it were within range of sight, the only conclusion to be drawn from the fact he had seen nothing so far was that the machines were still below the horizon.

The noise grew louder, reached a climax and diminished again. Ten minutes after Rhodan had first noticed it, it had disappeared again. "They're not on the right track yet," Rhodan smiled with relief. "I hope they don't find us for a long time!"

He looked at the sleeping Marshall. If the helicopters came closer he'd have to awaken him from his well-deserved slumber. They'd need every raygun if the chips were down. Furthermore, Marshall had to warn the seals so that they wouldn't be placed in jeopardy.

But there was no immediate danger.

More than 60 miles above this scene, someone else made a second and—for the time being—last attempt to intervene in the events taking place on Venus.

Reginald Bell, the battle-hardened companion of Perry Rhodan and Minister of Internal and External Security of the New Power, had heretofore been concerned with his own safety and was unable to come to the help of the others because the mighty positronic brain in the Venus fortress had enveloped the whole planet almost to the limit of its atmosphere in an impenetrable protective mantle that sealed it hermetically off from all outside influence.

Shortly after Rhodan had left, Bell took off from Terra in one of the spherical spaceships of the *Good Hope* class measuring 200 feet in diameter and officially called "Guppies" when they served as auxiliary vessels on board a larger battleship.

Thora had suffered a sort of mental short-circuit. Home sickness and the obsession that Rhodan didn't think of allowing her to return to Arkon, caused her to seek aid on Venus. The most important base of the New Power was located on Venus. Although it harbored no spaceships, it contained hyperwave radio transmitters with energy great enough to broadcast emergency signals that could reasonably be expected to be picked up by her people far out in space.

Thora had blasted off in one of the newly built destroyers and was shipwrecked on Venus when she approached the defense zone of the fortress because her ship had not yet been equipped with facilities to remit the code signal. Subsequently she was captured by Tomisenkov and both of them were in turn taken prisoner by Raskujan.

Rhodan followed her a few hours later but he and his two companions didn't fare any better than Thora. They had been able to avoid capture but their efforts to free Thora failed.

The third of the team was Reginald Bell. It was

presumably a simple matter for him in his *Guppy* to reach Venus without hindrance and to enter through the defense zone of the bulwark. With the technical gear available at the base he could have intervened in the battles, liberated Thora, rescued Rhodan and taught Raskujan a lesson to boot. The positronic brain, however, having been alarmed by the two previous unannounced flights, cordoned off Venus from the outer world and took over command of the fortress and the planet as a whole. As a consequence Bell was cruising with his spaceship outside the protective mantle and was not even in a position to communicate with Rhodan via radio. All electro-magnetic frequencies down to the long wavelengths of infra-red rays were blocked out.

Only once had Bell attempted to circumvent the barrier of the positronic brain by the deployment of a mutant, Tako Kakuta. The most remarkable of Tako Kakuta's amazing talents was teleportation. He was able to transport himself over distances up to 30,000 miles without recourse to technical conveyances. His medium for transport was the transcendental hyperspace. The method was thus equivalent to the transition of a spaceship with the exception of the energy source.

Tako had returned from his first attempt instantaneously and half dead. He himself was under the impression that he had been absent for hours. The fact of the matter was undoubtedly that the positronic brain was prepared to repulse infiltration attempts of any kind whatsoever, even those taking place on planes of a higher order. It was questionable that the base permanently maintained a five-dimensional defense screen around the whole planet. This would have required an immeasurable amount of energy. But apparently the positronic brain reacted to the intrusion of a super-body quickly enough to eject it again from its realm.

Tako Kakuta needed two days of Terrestrial time to recuperate.

On the following day Bell asked him whether he'd be willing to try it once more and gave a few reasons. "It's possible, for instance," Bell pointed out, "that the first failure was due to an accident. Perhaps you can get through to the fortress the second time without being molested. You remember that you once before entered the base with a tele-jump after Tomisenkov first landed with his armada of 500 spaceships and was scattered to the four winds with his crews. Of course, it's possible that the positronic brain considers the present situation much more dangerous than before and that it has therefore activated many more far-reaching defense measures. To be honest, it probably has. But shouldn't we try to make another attempt just the same?"

Bell spoke in gentle tones that ran counter to his usual custom. He was under no obligation to plead with a mutant or any other member of the New Power. In situations like the present it was his right to give orders.

But he knew what it meant to induce Tako Kakuta to undertake this task again. He had already reached the limit of his physical endurance the first time.

To his surprise Kakuta didn't hesitate for a moment. With an uncertain smile on his round child-like face he answered: "Of course I'll try again. I hope it won't be worse than the last time when I felt like being run over by an armored tank."

They prepared for the mission. Bell summoned two men of the crew to the command center and instructed them to hold Kakuta carefully when he reappeared in the ship.

Tako Kakuta took up his position. He exhibited a suffering mein and announced: "Here I go!"

The transition took less than a second. No sooner had they noticed his outline getting fuzzy than he had already completely vanished.

Reginald Bell held his breath. For an interval of two heartbeats he dared hope that this time their attempt had been successful. Then the Japanese suddenly re-appeared again.

His eyes were closed and his face distorted with pain. The men Bell had called to assist him, did their duty. The Japanese sank into their arms. He was unconscious.

'Take him to his cabin and watch him!" Bell ordered. "Let me know when he wakes up."

He turned around and stared at the observation screen filled with swirling, brightly lit masses of clouds.

The second attempt had failed miserably!

There were no more conceivable ways left for him to take a hand in the events on Venus. Rhodan had to carry on the struggle alone.

Son Okura saw the flat coast of the continent appear like a dark line.

Still 40 hours to midnight.

Marshall had woken up long ago and taken over Rhodan's post in order to give him a few minutes rest. Only Okura had been deprived of sleep the whole time. His eyes were still needed.

The seals pulled the boat steadily and reliably.

They had heard the helicopters a few more times. Each time the noise was a few decibels louder than previously. There could be little doubt that they were searching in sweeps either from south to north or in the opposite direction and that they were getting closer to the coast with each sweep, thereby nearing the fleeing boat more and more.

Marshall had warned the seals. They waited for his signal to slip out of the slings in case of attack and to swim away from the unsafe region. Marshall hoped that it wouldn't come to that but he was none too sure that he had any right for hope.

Rhodan got up again after his short rest and told the Japanese to lie down. Okura went to sleep and from then on they depended solely on their hearing. The eyes of the "ultra-sheer" were missing.

Shortly after 201 : 00 o'clock Venus time the observer of the leading unit of the helicopter squadron caught a tiny blip on his radar screen.

He notified the main flight group and learned that they had detected the same signal and it was determined that they had received a "true" reflex.

The precise position of the object was ascertained and it was found that it moved with considerable speed in a north-northeasterly direction.

Five minutes after the observation was made, the group of gunships veered east and steered with top velocity toward the unknown object which meanwhile had moved close to the coast of the peninsula.

The major in charge of the helicopter patrol felt certain that the observed object was somehow connected with the disappearance of the two lost machines. He instructed his observers to lock onto the blip in sight and to turn on the infra-red searchlight as soon as they came within range.

Rhodan listened attentively.

At first he heard only the usual steady hum of the distant aircraft as it approached from the south and reached a high point somewhere to the side of the boat. They then returned again. Closer but still outside the danger zone.

Rhodan waited for the sound to fade away north but it didn't happen. A new tone intermingled with the humming and caused a loud vibration.

Rhodan recognized what was going on in the darkness. The machines had discovered something, communicated among their units and coordinated their new course. For a few moments he hoped it wasn't their boat they had detected. The boat was made of resilient plastic which was not the most suitable material for the reflection of radar waves.

Yet when the noise began to grow with menacing speed, Rhodan knew that he was too optimistic. The radar instruments of the enemy were better than he had assumed. "Marshall! Wake up Son!"

Marshall had been listening too. He nodded and

went forward to arouse the Japanese. It wasn't very easy to do but he had no other choice under the circumstances.

"Son!" Rhodan called. "They're on the verge of attacking us. About 10 machines I'd guess. Keep your eyes open!"

And then: "Marshall!"

"Yes, sir!"

"Give the seals the alarm signal! Try to find out where we can take refuge if we survive the initial attack."

"Right away, sir!"

"Son!"

"Yes, sir!"

"How far are we from the coast?"

"Approximately 600 feet, sir!"

Rhodan uttered an angry curse. Why couldn't they've detected the boat a minute later?

Meanwhile Marshall had been busy. The seals slipped out of the ropes with extraordinary skill and sped away toward the shore. Marshall turned around and reported: "The seals are living in coastal caves which are half submerged in water and open to the sea. They said they'd admit us."

Rhodan nodded affirmatively. "Very good! Have your weapons ready!"

The buzzing of the helicopters had become more discernible. The ear was now able to differentiate between the high whistling of the engine jets and the whirring of the rotor blades. Son was soon able to inform them that he saw nine bright points approaching close to the surface of the water. "About one and a half miles," he added.

In the last few seconds before the seals abandoned the boat, they had pulled it about 150 feet closer to the coast. Now the distance was no more than 450 feet. Rhodan told his companions they'd have to swim the last stretch notwithstanding the peril posed by strange animals and plants hiding in the water.

"We'll blast the gunships with our fire on the first pass!" he said. "If our aim is good we should be able to shoot down one of their formations. That'll teach them some respect. The time they need to recover from their shock and regroup we can use to jump overboard and swim to shore. Carry the thermobeamer on your back and take at least one of the automatic pistols and plenty of ammunition with you. And above all try to reach the caves of the seals as quickly as possible. They can see us from the air when we're swimming in the water."

He had hardly finished speaking the last word when Okura raised his arm. "Caution! There's the infrared searchlight!"

Only the Japanese could perceive the concentrated beam of rays from the helicopter patrol scanning the surface of the ocean. The glittering reflexes of the infra-red light on the water were good reference points for Okura to estimate the time it would take until their boat was detected.

"Fifteen hundred feet!" he called. "They're coming straight toward us!"

That's no surprise, Rhodan thought. *All they have to do is to keep the radar blip in the center of the screen while they're flying. There's nothing to that.*

"Six hundred feet!" Okura shouted, covering his face with both hands. One of the searchlights had pinpointed the boat and blinded the Japanese although it was invisible to the others.

They had been discovered!

"Take cover!" Rhodan ordered.

The plastic walls of the boat offered a much more substantial cover than could be suspected at first glance. The synthetic material of the airtube was at least two and a half inches thick throughout. The collision with a bullet released heat which was used to draw the plastic material from the undamaged surroundings, thus sealing the hole. Any number of bullet holes and up to 15 hits by explosive shells could be rendered completely ineffective by this method. The 16th hit by an explosive shell would be something else again—

Out of the darkness an automatic cannon began a fusillade. The first burst fell short. About 50 feet over to the side Rhodan saw glittering water fountains spring up.

Okura threw up both arms as a sign that the helicopters had come within shooting range. Above the noise they heard Rhodan's voice yell: "Fire!"

It was uncanny, silent fire that leaped toward the hostile machines. Rhodan made out a whistling and clacking shadow at which he aimed the barrel of his impulse weapon, squeezing the trigger hard into the butt. He kept his eyes closed to avoid being blinded by the radiant beam of the energy discharge. He saw the glaring rays seize the big machine, deliver its entire energy to the body and installations of the craft and turn it with unrelenting rapidity into a lump of melting and steaming metal that finally exploded in a loud detonation on impact with the water.

The same spectacle happened at two more places. Rhodan was elated by a feeling of triumph when he saw the other machines turn tail and retreat with howling engines.

"All ready for a swim?" he shouted.

"Ready!" he heard Okura's voice.

"Ready!" Marshall chimed in.

"Let's go!"

They went over the side of the boat, hit the water with a splash and started to swim vigorously. The water was slimy and viscous but they made good headway and stayed together by calling out to each other from time to time.

This time the ugly rat-a-tat-tat of the machineguns sounded pleasantly far away. *They're attacking the boat for a second time*, Rhodan noted with relief.

He heard some hissing and crackling and saw a shower of sparks sprayed across the water as one of the projectiles blew up the depot of ammunition in the boat. Virtually at the same instant, the helicopters ceased their fire. They probably were of the opinion that it was impossible for anyone to survive such an explosion.

Okura called over that two of the 'copters hovered low over the boat's debris.

"You better swim a little faster!" Rhodan called back. "They'll soon find out we got away. How much farther, Son?"

"Two hundred feet, sir!"

He tried to test how deep the ocean was but it was almost impossible to get his legs down in the water.

Then Okura's voice roared: "Look out. They're coming!"

The vehicles approached slowly. They had not yet determined where the crew of the boat had fled. They played their infra-red beams over the water and probed for the elusive defenders.

Rhodan guessed that they were still 120 feet from the shore and that the helicopters had come within 300 feet behind them.

Marshall suddenly exclaimed: "Solid ground! From here on we can walk."

Rhodan swam toward the voice. He saw Marshall's waving arms appear from the dark and let his feet sink down till he touched bottom.

Walking wasn't much faster but it was easier. Step by step they got closer to the coast, which began to emerge as a black line in the dark night. Meanwhile the helicopter also came constantly nearer. Rhodan heard the Japanese groan abruptly: "They spotted us!"

Rhodan was unable to see the cone of the searchlight but he could hear the chattering of the machineguns. The bullets plopped a few feet to the right into the water.

"We've almost reached the seals!" Marshall called above the noise. "They're straight ahead of us!"

The gunship corrected its aim. Rhodan observed the splashing tracks of the shots wander toward himself. They were closing in within 15 feet.

He stumbled over something and fell head first into the water. He was grabbed hard by the shoulder and put back on his feet. Up front Marshall shouted something he didn't understand. His voice sounded peculiar and hollow.

The cave! Marshall was already inside the cave. Rhodan watched the squirts of water whipped up by the machinegun fire pass behind him. With a feeling of indescribable relief he staggered across the smooth ground covered with water and noticed that it was slightly climbing. Finally he reached a slab of stone protruding a few inches from the water. Marshall was sitting on top of it and waving to him. The Japanese was about to clamber up from the other side.

Marshall helped Rhodan get out of the water. Rhodan pulled his legs up and stretched out on his back, deeply inhaling the damp musty air in the cave of the seals.

Outside the machineguns of the helicopters kept rattling on. But the entrance to the cave was much too small and filled high with water. It effectively prevented the enemy from doing any harm to the fugitives.

Chapter Three

TERROR OF THE TYREX

"Have you made up your mind?" Tomisenkov asked.

Thora was startled when she discovered him crawling under the wall into her tent. However, she kept her composure in spite of it. "I've decided to cooperate with you," she said with all the dignity she could muster, "if you can convince me that there's any hope for success."

Tominsenkov sat down uninvited and gazed at her with narrow eyes. "I can guarantee you that you and I and a few of my men can leave the camp unmolested and that we can advance a few hundred yards into the jungle. What happens next, however, depends on what you or your fabled Venusian fortress can do to protect us from Raskujan's helicopters and soldiers."

Thora's reddish eyes lit up suspiciously. "If you believe that I'd allow you to walk into the base as easily as that, you're badly mistaken ..."

Tomisenkov gestured angrily. "The time for that has passed," he assured her. "I'm no longer interested in conquering the bulwark. I can live without it."

"And what are you interested in now?" Thora asked, not without scorn.

Tomisenkov looked at her and answered earnestly: "I desire to prevent a fool from raising havoc on Venus. You don't know us humans very well, do you?"

"I've never bothered to learn much about you," Thora replied stiffly.

This didn't hurt Tomisenkov's feelings. "You ought to make up for this neglect at the first occasion. We're an interesting race. Living for one year on Venus with the bare necessities was sufficient for me and most of my men, for example, to learn to love this ugly and horrid world. We're the first ones to have existed on Venus for a whole year without homes, soft beds and similar amenities, roaming the jungles, mountain valleys and always living in trees. Venus is *ours*— and we're now *Venusians* or whatever you want to call it. That's why I'm no longer interested in your base and why I want to make it impossible for Raskujan to play dictator. Can you understand this?"

Thora gave no direct answer. "Very well," she finally said. "We'll leave the camp together. I can't make you any promises. But under the circumstances our flight could look like ..."

Rhodan allowed himself only a few minutes to catch his breath. Then he raised himself up. "Marshall, tell the seals they must leave the cave as quickly as possible."

The helicopters had departed. Quiet reigned in the cave, broken only by the lapping waves and the scraping of the seals' flippers on the wet rock in the background.

Marshall advised the seals of the warning. "They don't understand why it's necessary to vacate their cavern," he told Rhodan.

"Because the helicopters will hurry back to throw a few bombs at us."

Marshall transmitted his words although it was

difficult to describe the concept of a bomb to the seals. "Agreed," he finally said. "Does this cave have an exit on land?" Rhodan inquired.

Marshall asked the seals. "Yes, there's an escape hole. A passage leads upwards and ends in the middle of the jungle."

"Excellent. We'll use it to get out. I think Raskujan has left one of the machines behind to watch the surroundings. If we can disappear unseen, it'll be a great advantage."

Rhodan estimated the radius of the danger zone to be expected from the bombs and let Marshall explain to the seals how far they should go away from the cavern in order to stay safe. It turned out that this was no trouble at all for the seals. They were by nature wandering animals and there were more than a thousand caves lining the coast. They promised to warn other families of seals to shun the hazardous area.

Marshall also took the additional precautionary measure of alarming all seals in the vicinity by telepathic calls. Finally he tried to convey the feeling to the seals that Rhodan was grateful for the help they had received and would be happy to do anything in his power for them.

Surprisingly, the seals had no wishes. Their needs were small and Venus was a generous world for them. They took leave in a somewhat awkward manner due to their different mentalities and assured each other of their friendship.

Then Rhodan and his companions departed. They crawled on their knees through a 300 foot long passage smelling of fish and blubber and reached the outside at 202:00 o'clock some distance away from the coast and under the dense cover of the jungle where they couldn't be seen.

Marshall had obtained a rough description of the territory from the seals.

The topography of the seals was no exact science but Rhodan was able to determine that the place where the northern continent joined the peninsula was between five and ten miles away from their present location.

"Very well," he stated. "A maximum distance of 10 miles to the juncture. The defense screen of the bulwark begins about 12 miles north of the coast. At most a distance of 22 miles together to the defense screen. There we should be able to activate the identification process of the positronic brain. And then," he said with a tired smile, "the worst will be behind us!"

Corporal Wlassow came stomping out of the darkness in a great rush. "I need help," he panted. "Tomisenkov is gone!"

Five guards were posted at the gate of the primitive prisoner camp. A sergeant was in charge. He gave Wlassow two men to aid him in the search for the escaped general and told him: 'I'll give you 15 minutes to find Tomisenkov. Then I'll have to make a report."

Wlassow nodded and ran with his two comrades back into the darkness. One of the guards switched on a flashlight but Wlassow hit him over the arm. "Turn it off!" he snarled. "Do you want him to see us coming? That's no way to catch him."

The argument seemed reasonable, the more so since Wlassow could have found his way to Tomisenkov's tent blindfolded. He marched ahead and paid no attention as some shadowy figures sprang suddenly out of the dark, leaped at the throats of his comrades and choked them till they lost consciousness.

"O.K.," a voice whispered in the darkness. "Let's strip them!"

Wlassow turned around and took a few steps back. Two men were busy taking off the unconscious guards' uniforms. "Take your time," Wlassow said calmly. "We've got 15 minutes before the sergeant gives the alarm."

The two sentries were tied up, gagged and hidden in the bushes. The camp was safe from wild animals —except from big ants. Assuming that the ants didn't invade the camp in the next hour, the two men were not in danger of their lives.

A stocky, powerful shadow rose from the darkness and gave Wlassow a hearty slap on the shoulder. "Well done, my boy," Tomisenkov said admiringly.

Wlassow grinned with embarrassment. "I feel a little uneasy about it," he replied.

Tomisenkov made a brushing gesture with his hand. "You'll soon get over that," he added quickly.

One of the other men said: "We're ready chief!"

"O.K. Is everybody here? Wlassow, Alicharin, Breshnjew, Zelinskij, Thora?"

"All present, chief!"

Tomisenkov nodded. "Very well, let's go!"

The sergeant at the gate didn't become suspicious when Wlassow returned so soon with two men whose faces couldn't be recognized. His companions were clad in the neat uniforms which distinguished Raskujan's troops in contrast to the ragged clothing of the soldiers from the Space Landing Division.

"Is everything in order?" the sergeant asked.

"Yes. He crawled out under the wall of the tent and took a walk. I don't believe. . . ."

He didn't have to say any more. He had reached the sergeant. Quick as a flash he lifted the hand holding the heavy service revolver and hit the sergeant hard over the head with the butt. Wlassow caught the large body of the man and put him gently down on the grass.

One of the other guards stuck his head out of the rough guardhouse. "What's the mater? What happened to . . ."

"Come here! He suddenly collapsed."

Unsuspecting, the guard came over to help Wlassow. As he bent over the unconscious figure he also was struck a hard blow on the head so that he fell on the limp body of the unconscious sergeant.

Wlassow made short shrift of the last guard. He entered the guardhouse with his gun drawn. The man stared at him sleepily. "Get up and raise your hands!" Wlassow ordered. Sleepy and terrified, the man obeyed.

"Go out the door in front of me," Wlassow continued. The soldier complied. When he stepped through the door, he was whacked over the head by one of Tomisenkov's men and fell to the ground like his two comrades. Wlassow whistled twice. There was a stirring in the darkness and Tomisenkov, Alicharin and Thora came out.

"Tie them up, gag them and take their weapons," Tomisenkov ordered curtly. They worked fast. The three unconscious men were also concealed in the bushes at some distance from the guardhouse. They thereby hoped to delay the search for the fugitives until the next inspection patrol had found the missing guards.

Altogether seven sentries had been overwhelmed and removed. One in front of Thora's tent and one at the tent in which Alicharin, Breshnjew and Zelinskij had been held together; the two guards assigned to Wlassow by the sergeant and finally the sergeant himself and his two comrades. The eighth of the missing guards would puzzle the patrol: Wlassow. It was difficult to believe that one of Raskujan's soldiers would give up the security of the rocket post to follow a man, marked as a renegade in Raskujan's political vernacular into poverty and peril.

Perhaps doubts like these would delay the beginning of the pursuit for a few more minutes.

With Tomisenkov at the head the little group passed through the wide open gate of the camp. Wlassow, loaded down with two automatic pistols and plenty of ammunition, formed the rearguard and closed the gate carefully.

Tomisenkov turned northeast in order to get around the well-guarded landing pad for the rockets. Five minutes later they reached the edge of the jungle at the side of the swath drawn through the forest by the *Stardust* a year ago.

Wlassow was informed of Tomisenkov's plan to reach as quickly as possible the protective screen of the New Power's Venusian base. The idea of stealing a helicopter was dropped immediately. A helicopter could not be started without being noticed. Raskujan's men would be on their heels within a few minutes and with a ratio of twenty to one the outcome of the chase could easily be foreseen.

They just as quickly abandoned a plan to use the burned-out path for their escape so as to advance more swiftly. This was exactly what Raskujan would have anticipated. By choosing to make their way through the jungle, they not only misled Raskujan but were at the same time well-protected from discovery by sight.

Tomisenkov was certain that his flight wouldn't be detected before two hours when the next inspection patrol passed by. He also knew from his year of experience on Venus that a path broken through the jungle would grow over no later than 90 minutes so that their pursuers would be unable to tell it from the untouched jungle. As far as Tomisenkov was concerned, he had solved all his problems with a maximum of reliability. He was reasonably well convinced that only such circumstances as were impossible to predict could lead to the detection and capture of his group as long as he was guiding it.

The question of final success was a different matter. Wlassow didn't understand what the Arkonide woman had in mind, having received only second hand information from Tomisenkov. It had something to do with the defense screen against which Raskujan had vainly butted his head every day for a year. Thora seemed to know the special function by which the barrier was held in position and this would enable her and her companions to enter the terrain of the base by applying the appropriate methods.

But it was over Wlassow's head and he simply trusted Tomisenkov's knowledge. If Tomisenkov saw a chance of success in Thora's plans, he was likely to have valid reasons for his optimism.

They had traveled a distance of one and a half miles from the exit of the shaft when a bomb exploded. The forest was illuminated for a few seconds by a pale light which was clearly noticeable through the dense roof of leaves. Half a minute later the shockwave of the explosion rolled over the land.

They were not affected by the blast. It was a small fusion bomb with a non-critical split mass, reaching the critical factor of one at the time of ignition by utilizing a suitable reflector such as graphite or beryllium-oxide. The dangerous radioactivity was confined to the immediate proximity of the explosion. The cave of the seals, which had served as their haven for a few minutes, and its surroundings in 1500 foot radius, would be a contaminated area for some time, but if the seals heeded the warning they wouldn't be hurt by the despicable bombing.

Nonetheless, the deployment of an atomic bomb was additional proof for Perry Rhodan that it would be criminal irresponsibility to leave Venus to the mercy of people like Colonel Raskujan. They treated Venus like an outpost of Terra. They failed to understand that a new world called for new methods. It was beyond their comprehension that the international rivalry on which politics between the countries on

Terra was based, could not be allowed to be transplanted and continued on Venus.

What these people lacked was "cosmic thinking" as Perry Rhodan had come to term it.

Rhodan felt it extremely regrettable that so far he had been prevented from putting Raskujan in his place.

Of the 22 miles to the perimeter of the defense screen less than two had now been covered. Time for an extended rest had to be taken out in the next five hours or their legs and senses would give out.

They spent the pause in the highest and least hazardous level of the forest. Son Okura selected a tree promising comparative comfort and security. With some difficulty he reached—at a height of about 120 feet—a fork in the tree big enough to offer a safe place for all of them in its hollow. Rhodan volunteered to take the first watch of two hours. Then it was the turn of the Japanese, with John Marshall completing the cycle.

They settled down as best they could and both Marshall and Okura were fast asleep in a minute. Rhodan, however, used the time to ponder some of the problems that had so far remained unsolved.

A year ago he had deprived general Tomisenkov's hostile Space Landing Division of their ships and driven them into the forest with the intention of creating from Tomisenkov's 10,000 men—or rather what was left of them—the first stock of inhabitants of Venus. The plan had proceeded very well. Tomisenkov's division had split up as expected. Ideological splinter groups formed, such as the pacifists under

Lieutenant Wallerinski. The separation had not taken place without inner conflicts. There had been some fighting. But the groups had established themselves, most of them on the rocky islands rising from the dense murderous jungle, which offered a good view and a semblance of security.

However, in the meantime Colonel Raskujan had landed with his fleet of supplies. For one year he had tried to conquer the base of the New Power and thus had unknowingly given time to Tomisenkov and his followers to adjust to life on Venus. Then came the fateful moment when Raskujan learned that remnants of the Space Landing Division had survived and he set out to subjugate them and achieve the designs dictated by his lust for power.

At any rate, Raskujan was a serious stumbling block. He had to be eliminated lest he cause even greater damage. There was only one important contribution Raskujan's fleet could make: A major part of the crew consisted of women, who were an essential requirement for forming a biologically balanced community. In every other respect Raskujan's presence was detrimental.

In Rhodan's opinion, Tomisenkov was the man capable of developing a thriving colony. This belief was untainted by feelings of a personal nature. Rhodan was uncertain whether he could ever form a close relationship with Tomisenkov. He knew the man only from reports by the prisoners he had made a year ago. The image they reflected was not overly pleasant or harmonious. But Rhodan gave Tomisenkov credit, as long as he had not personally met him, that a year on

Venus had made a wiser and humbler man of him.

When he had arrived at this point in his train of thought, he heard an intermittent rustling noise among the multitude of sounds emanating from the jungle at all times. It seemed to come from close by. Rhodan retreated behind the cover of the branches and watched. His eyes used to the darkness, he was able to see a distance of about 10 feet, sufficient to keep any menace away with his impulse-beamer.

A long narrow object slid into view from above. For awhile it dangled aimlessly between the branches. Then it lurched down and grew bigger, dragging an elastic lump with constantly changing shape behind it and descending on a track of self-produced slime along the huge trunk of the tree.

Rhodan knew the animal. It was one of the land-bound mollusks living on Venus that built caves in the ground as traps and went hunting when their appetite was unsatisfied by the victims in their pits.

Rhodan waited impatiently. He knew it was useless to shoot at the single tentacle dangling close before his eyes.

The spongy body of the mollusk was covered with a leathery skin on the greater part of its epidermis. It kept in hiding for awhile behind the foliage. Then it continued slithering and scraping down the trunk of the tree, stopped again, then lunged with its swinging tentacle to seize its prey.

Rhodan held still as the repulsive scaly arm glided over his head to his right shoulder and began to hug him around his hip. He'd already slowly raised his impulse-beamer and carefully aimed the barrel at the thick lump of the beast's body. He planted both feet against a branch of the fork and when the mollusk began to jerk him from his seat, he fired.

As it was necessary with a thermo-gun, his shot was highly accurate. The blinding beam hit the body of the mollusk at the farthest point from the trunk. The substance of the animal burned and steamed as it hissed and sprayed a yellow shower of sparks into the dark jungle. Rhodan could feel the strength of the tentacle ebbing away. The mollusk loosened its grip and fell, falling victim to the heat he had generated with his shot.

A few seconds later only a scorched spot on the bark of the tree remained as a reminder of the danger that had threatened the three in the fork of the branches.

Rhodan chose another place to sit and kept watching. Incidents of this sort were rather rare at their height above the ground. There was no likelihood that their rest would be disturbed again during his watch.

He leaned back and returned to his thoughts. He contemplated different endeavor toward the foundation and furthering of a new colony on Venus—providing he came out of *this* venture alive.

The camp ground was primitive but nobody except Thora was bothered by it and even she was careful not to complain.

They lay quietly on the moist ground and dozed. Only Tomisenkov was still alert. He talked to Thora about the prospects of gaining access to the fortress through the defense barrier.

"The way I understand it," Tomisenkov began, "you're hopeful that the positronic brain in the fortress will recognize your identity and grant your admittance. Is this right?"

Thora nodded a little reluctantly. "Yes, but I can't be absolutely sure," she answered. "As far as I can judge the situation, the positronic brain has assumed exclusive control of the base as a result of various menacing incidents. This means that the method of sending an agreed code signal with a special transmitter, by which a member of the New Power was authorized to enter the base, has been suspended. This is fortunate for us since we don't have such a code-transmitter and no means of building one.

"As a consequence, we'll have to depend on the positronic brain identifying my brain-waves as those of an authorized person once we've reached the border of the protective screen."

She looked at Tomisenkov and he was surprised by the expression of helplessness in her eyes. "Unfortunately I don't know whether the positronic brain will recognize me as an authorized person. If Perry Rhodan were with us, there could be no doubt of our success. But alone ..." She left the end of the sentence unspoken. Tomisenkov felt the urge to console her. But before he could think of something appropriate to say, his attention was suddenly completely diverted and concentrated on another matter.

Thora didn't know what had happened. She had heard nothing.

"Alicharin!" Tomisenkov called.

"Yes, chief!" answered the little slant-eyed man.

"I heard it. It's a tyrex." He said it indifferently, almost bored.

"It's coming from east-north-east," Zelinskij added. And Breshnjew observed: "It seems to head straight for the swamp." Tomisenkov nodded. "Keep quiet, boys. Maybe it'll pass us by."

The answering voices from the darkness agreed.

"What is it?" Thora asked excitedly. "A dinosaur?"

"Yes. Can't you hear it?"

"If you mean the thump it makes every minute," she finally said, "then ..."

"It's not a minute," Tomisenkov replied smilingly. "It's between 30 and 40 seconds."

"And why do you call it a tyrex?"

"Because I'd be out of breath—perhaps eaten up? —if I stopped to call it by its proper paleolontological name every time: *Tyrannosarus Rex* ... King of the great prehistoric reptiles and the only flesh-eater among the dinosaurs. It devours everything that comes its way as long as it's an animal. It'll even attack other saurians, sometimes larger than itself. Of course it can't always consume them completely. It tears out the best pieces and leaves the rest to the ants."

Thora listened breathlessly. "And why does it walk so slowly?"

"Slowly?" Tomisenkov laughed loudly. "It moves at 12 miles an hour. It's the only saurian walking upright most of the time. The forelegs are seldom used for anything other than holding its prey. It isn't as big as the largest dinosaurs but it towers at least 30 feet above them as it walks erect. Its legs are almost 50 feet long. Figure out how many steps per minute it must take to maintain a velocity of 12 miles per hour. It's no more than one and a half or two!"

Thora understood.

The thumping earth-shaking steps grew louder. Simultaneously the other sounds in the jungle swelled up with it. The animals were fleeing before the monster.

"Are we going to sit here till he tramples us into the ground?" Thora asked with apprehension.

"Where do you want us to go?" Tomisenkov countered her question.

Thora pointed uncertainly into the darkness. "*There* —away from *here*!"

"And how do you know it won't pass where you want to hide? Can you decide which direction it'll take?"

Thora shook her head in bafflement.

"Besides, you needn't worry about being trampled," Tomisenkov continued.

"Why not?"

"A tyrex doesn't trample what it can *eat*. And it's got a damn good nose to smell its prey. You can depend on that!"

He left Thora with this "consolation" and crawled over to Alicharin who had cleared a spot of ground of all plants and pressed his ear to it so he could listen better. "How's it coming?" Tomisenkov asked.

Alicharin frowned. "Not very well. At best it'll pass at a distance of 150 feet from us."

Tomisenkov became alarmed. "One hundred fifty feet is nothing," he growled. "It can smell us three times as far."

Alicharin nodded.

Tomisenkov turned around. "Take up your positions behind the trees, boys! And shoot straight!"

He saw Wlassow standing at the side, not knowing what to do. "Don't stand around!" Tomisenkov told him. "It's a tyrex and it's going to swallow you up when it gets you in its paws. Breshnjew will show you how to lie in wait for a tyrex. And remember one thing: if its head comes down to look at you, shoot it in the eye. It's virtually the only spot where it's vulnerable. Got it?"

"Yes," Wlassow replied with a lump in his throat.

Alicharin remained at his listening post to the last minute. Tomisenkov had meanwhile picked a tree as cover and waved to Alicharin when he finished listening.

Alicharin slipped behind the cover and put his automatic pistol beside him. "It won't pass more than 60 feet from us," he panted. "It'll pick up our scent in three or four minutes."

Tomisenkov merely nodded. And then—between two of the mighty rumbling steps of the dinosaur—he heard another noise. He was vexed and it took some time before he realized that his ears were not deceiving him.

In the excitement over the tyrex he had practically forgotten about Raskujan.

Tomisenkov started to laugh and Alicharin, who had also recognized the noise, joined in the laughter.

"Good grief!" Tomisenkov gasped. "If they don't

watch out the tyrex is going to gulp them down, helicopter and all!"

It was a single machine with a regular two man crew, a lieutenant and a sergeant. The sergeant piloted the craft and the lieutenant acted as observer. Awhile ago the lieutenant had muttered: "I'd like to know how anyone can find people in this matted jungle."

And now he detected something in the oscillating beam of his infra-red searchlight that had nothing to do with the hunted men but nevertheless occupied his full attention: A sturdy powerful neck towering at least 30 feet above the roof of the jungle and topped by a huge, wide-mouthed head swaying slowly to and fro on the column of the neck.

He ordered the sergeant to pull the machine up at least 150 feet higher and to hover in the air. The sergeant had also noticed the dinosaur through his blind-flying instrument, an infra-red set mounted in the vehicle. He complied at once with the order and remained at a safe altitude, about 250 feet from the beast.

"It stopped, too," the lieutenant stated. "But it shows no interest in us. It seems to have discovered something else!"

Tomisenkov looked for Thora. She was also hidden behind a tree and held one of the spare automatic pistols in her hand. Tomisenkov could see her white-blond hair shine in the darkness. "Just stay still!" he called to her. "We can handle it ourselves."

Thora replied mockingly: "Don't worry about me!

I only want to find out how much your old-fashioned shooting irons are worth."

With an admiring growl Tomisenkov turned around again. At this moment the crashing and rumbling noises the dinosaur created on his march through the jungle ceased. Tomisenkov whistled through his teeth.

"It's got wind of us!" Alicharin declared.

Tomisenkov raised himself up on his arms and called into the night: "It's found us, boys! It won't be long now!" Half-subconsciously it registered that the helicopter had also stopped moving. It hovered above the crowns of the trees and seemed to watch the dinosaur.

Wlassow felt scared. He didn't like to wait in the darkness for the aggressive behemoth, not even knowing what it looked like. Wlassow lay behind a huge tree as Breshnjew had advised him but Breshnjew himself was lying so far away that Wlassow couldn't even see him. He heard Tomisenkov's shouted warning and gripped his weapon tighter. In addition to the bullet clip in his gun he kept 10 more clips on the ground beside him within reach.

Then the scene suddenly started to move. Wlassow heard a strong whizzing sound, then a din of crashing trees as if the dinosaur had started to push forward again. Instinctively Wlassow waited for the thump of the next step.

But it failed to come. It was almost too late when he realized that the dinosaur had merely moved its neck. He heard the breaking of the branches and saw a huge shadow close above him. From one breath to the next the air was pervaded with a beastly stench. Wlassow heard quick furious hissing as the dinosaur exhaled —and then the tremendous head emerged from the darkness.

For a second Wlassow's blood froze in his veins. Not in his wildest dreams had he ever before seen such an ugly and ferocious sight. He saw a mouth with two double rows of sharp teeth lunging toward him, a paw so big that he could have stood up in it. Somewhere from left and right the swift grabbing forelegs slashed through the brush. Finally his terrified gaze was caught by the round iridescent eyes of the monster staring intently at him from a distance of 10 feet.

Suddenly Wlassow remembered the advice Tomisenkov and Breshnjew had given him. He jerked up his automatic pistol, aimed carefully at the left eye and fired.

A salvo of small explosive bullets hit the target. The horrible face of the dinosaur disappeared at once and a second later such a stupendous ear-splitting roar came from up above that Wlassow dropped his gun and pressed his hands against his ears.

"Now!" the lieutenant yelled excitedly. "Now it's seizing its prey!"

He watched through the infra-red filter how the colossal animal lowered its neck and dropped its head down into the foliage. For a moment he saw only the scaly base of its neck. Then the head jerked up again with wide open jaws. And what a head it was!

At the place where the left eye had been gaped a deep jagged hole from which blood was spurting in streams. At first the lieutenant couldn't understand what animal was able to inflict such a terrible wound on the huge beast. He waited wide-eyed for a few moments for a second dinosaur to pop up from the darkness and continue mangling the first one.

But this failed to materialize. The savage wounded creature kept howling; turned at last to the side and staggered away.

And then it suddenly dawned on the lieutenant. A well-placed volley of explosive bullets such as used in automatic pistols was capable of inflicting the hideous wound.

He barked his orders so sharply and unexpectedly that he startled the sergeant: "Down lower! Search the terrain where the dinosaur stopped!"

The sergeant obeyed. He dived down steeply and skimmed over the treetops. The enormous bulk of the dinosaur had broken a wide path through the jungle and the lieutenant directed his searchlight toward the spot where it veered sharply from its initial direction. The pilot held the machine steady and the lieutenant in his eagerness didn't realize the risk he was taking.

Tomisenkov was aware of the possible dangers that could evolve from the situation. Although he didn't know what had alerted the helicopter he had no doubts that it was chasing the fugitives. He shouted from his hiding place: "Nobody move till the 'copter leaves!"

But his shout didn't reach Wlassow's ears above the blasting jets and Wlassow probably wouldn't have paid any attention anyway: He was in the throes of an indescribable mood—a psychotic mixture of victorious frenzy and the after-effect of the horrible fright he had endured. With a wide leap he jumped into the path torn by the dinosaur, pointed his pistol at the clearly recognizable shadow of the helicopter and pulled the trigger. His salvo hit the plexiglass cockpit of the machine squarely.

The sergeant was killed instantly and the lieutenant, so far unhurt, realized at once what happened. Without trying to take over the controls of the aircraft, which retained its altitude for a few seconds, he grabbed the microphone of the still-operative radio and shouted his report. He was still talking when the machine toppled over and plummeted like a rock into the middle of the dinosaur's trail, bursting with a thunderous clap.

The radio station at Raskujan's post received the report: "Located fugitives! About two miles northeast of camp ..." Then nothing but a weak tapping—the faint by-product of the thunderous explosion reaching the radio officer over the waves.

The officer was an experienced radio man. He could deduce the meaning of the sudden interruption of the agonized screaming. No doubt Colonel Raskujan would attach the greatest importance to the message.

He contacted the command center of the flagship and advised Colonel Raskujan of the call he had received.

Chapter Four

MENACE OF THE ANTS

Wlassow seemed to be protected by a benign fate. Leaping like a panther, he had thrown himself down far enough away and just in time to escape the dreadful force of the fiery detonation. He landed in a stinking bush with moist twigs which immediately began to wind themselves around his body. The shockwave that followed freed him of the unwanted embrace and carried him a few feet farther without inflicting other damage than some scratches on his face and hands.

The forest had suddenly fallen quiet after the furious events of the past minutes.

Wlassow could hear the blood coursing in his ears before Tomisenkov's irate voice reached him: "Who's the fool who shot at the helicopter?"

Wlassow raised himself up and tested his limbs. "I did!" he exclaimed. Then he started to walk back. Somebody had turned on a half-concealed flashlight to light up the ground. It was Tomisenkov. Alicharin and Zelinskij stood beside him. Breshnjew and Thora appeared from the undergrowth.

"Didn't you hear me order everybody to freeze?" Tomisenkov growled.

"No," Wlassow replied truthfully and puzzled.

"What were you thinking of when you shot at the helicopter?"

The question was even more baffling for Wlassow.

"Well," he answered hesitantly, "I thought the same as any other machine gunner would, shooting at a hostile aircraft. I can't find anything wrong ..."

Tomisenkov didn't let him finish. "So you can't find anything wrong with it!" he shouted angrily. "Don't you know the men in that machine could send a call back before they were knocked out?"

"In such a short time...!" Wlassow was skeptical.

"In such a short time!" Tomisenkov mocked. "And suppose they made *no* report, Raskujan will miss them no later than in half an hour and send another chopper to look for them. It's only a matter of minutes to find this mass of metal by radar. Everything we've done so far has been ruined. Raskujan won't have to pick up our track at the camp to follow us, he can start right here."

Wlassow stood with drooping shoulders. A few moments ago he had considered himself the hero of the day, now he felt a dumb clod: disgraced.

"I can see it now," he mumbled dejectedly. "What can I do about it?"

"There's nothing you can do now! You'll have to get moving in double time just like the rest of us."

Tomisenkov turned around and looked at Thora and Breshnjew. "If Raskujan didn't know where we're heading, he knows it now. We can't go on marching northeast. We'll have to proceed to the southeast and try to mislead his helicopters. This means a detour and it's a great nuisance for us but we've got no other choice. Let's go!"

In great haste they scurried eastward along the swath cut by the wounded dinosaur that had meanwhile disappeared in the depth of the jungle. They used a small gap in the thicket to penetrate once more into the dark forest.

Tomisenkov assumed again, as he had the first time, that Raskujan's men would begin to look for the escaped prisoners in the broad trampled down lane. With luck their maneuver could help them avoid the pursuing helicopters.

A few minutes past 213:00 o'clock Perry Rhodan and his companions reached the edge of a swamp stretching—much to their discomfort—as far as the eye could see to left and right.

Rhodan had learned enough from his experience with Venusian swamps that he didn't even consider for a moment walking around the treacherous terrain. He asked Son to investigate the trees in the swamp and decided they were satisfactory.

"We'll swing through the trees over the swamp," Rhodan told them. "Son, you take the lead! Marshall, keep your eyes open. One wrong step or missed grip and you'll have had it."

They clambered up the trees on some vines. Okura led the way and set the pace because he was the only one who could see in the darkness and was also the most handicapped of the three. Okura had a birth defect that impeded his walking. Though he always endeavored to keep pace with other people, there were occasions—such as the present one—when he was forced to slow down by his encumbrance. Despite their extended rest they were all close to the breaking point and Okura felt it worst.

However, Rhodan didn't fare much better. There was no time to take care of the wound in his shoulder. He felt the injury throbbing again and his blood running hotter through his veins than before. The damp air of the jungle was laden with bacteria and his wound was bound to start festering or he would get a fever.

Perhaps both!

He knew that it was time to take a 30 hour rest to recuperate from the hardships which had abused their bodies. But 30 hours were too valuable at this time to be used for repose.

Thora was in danger and with her the Venusian base as well. Although Rhodan had great respect for Thora's resoluteness, there was a grave possibility that she would be unable to withstand indefinitely the inquisitionary methods of Raskujan. And even if she didn't give Raskujan information enabling him to gain immediate access to the bulwark, he had a great number of capable technicians and electronics experts available who would reap more knowledge from Thora's allusions to the workings of the positronic brain in particular and the structure of the base in general than the New Power would want them to have in their possession.

Therefore, Thora had to be freed. And since the liberation of Thora from the heavily guarded post was, without adequate means, likely to be doomed to failure from the outset, it was imperative that Rhodan first remove the barrier of the positronic brain so that he could obtain the necessary equipment.

This didn't pose any undue difficulties except that

they had to take into account the considerable distance separating them from the circumference of the defense screen girdling the fortress.

It was impossible for Rhodan to identify himself before reaching the border of the field. He had no practical means permitting him communications across a long distance. Only when he faced the protective mantle would the positronic brain examine him and determine that he was the one for whom the fortress opened its gates at all times. From then on everything else would be easy going.

The quagmire below them strained their patience. Since the Japanese, too, was unable to look through the dense foliage, they had to cut off a piece of a branch from time to time, clean away the leaves and drop it down, listening to the sound of its impact to guess the kind of surface it was.

For hours on end they heard only the splash of the weighty object landing in the heavy morass.

Rhodan was fully aware that the whole undertaking would have been an act of folly without the mutant ability of Son Okura. At 217:00 o'clock they stopped for another break. Rhodan would have very much preferred to go on a few hundred feet more because Okura claimed that the trees farther ahead were much closer together than where they had stopped, leading him to the conclusion that the swamp ended there. But by that time nobody was able to lift a leg, let alone move along a vine stretched between trees with the whole weight of his body hanging from his hands.

The swamp was sufficiently devoid of animals climbing about in the trees for Rhodan to deem it unnecessary to set up a watch. All three of them fell into a deep coma-like sleep—till they were suddenly awakened by a noise, not because it was very loud but rather because it was so uncommon in these surroundings.

The whistling of helicopter engines and the rattling of machineguns!

It was too far away to have been meant for them. The sound came from northwest and Raskujan's gunships seemed to have detected something there to shoot at.

Rhodan looked at his watch—set for Terrestrial time and saw that about three hours had passed since they interrupted their journey. It was shortly before 220:00 o'clock.

Although the shooting soon ceased and the helicopters flew away, Rhodan was interested to know what had caused the commotion. The origin of the noise was in the direction of their march anyway. The three hours of rest had sufficiently restored their strength—at least temporarily—so that they were able to leave at once.

Son Okura's conclusion proved to be correct. A few minutes after their departure they noticed that the ground below was solid again. They climbed down and thereafter made better time.

Half an hour later the terrain began to rise. They had reached the foothills of the mountains and regarded it as a friendly fate. The mountain they were approaching was the same one where the fortress was located.

* * *

They constantly heard the helicopters whirring above them, sometimes close over their heads and sometimes a little farther away.

Raskujan's men had found the burned out metal pile of the gunship shot down by Wlassow just as Tomisenkov and his group slipped into the jungle. As Tomisenkov had foreseen, they first flew along the path broken by the dinosaur, scouring it for the fugitives. When this proved fruitless they changed their tactic and drew wide circles over the land, stopping at regular intervals to lower a man on a cable with a winch to look around below the roof of leaves.

Tomisenkov kept his little band together. Finally the terrain began to rise, at first gently and comfortably and then suddenly at such a steep angle that it required the skill of mountain climbers to ascend. Using their hands and feet they climbed up step by step on a $70°$ wall that was well overgrown with bushes and trees. At the top Tomisenkov expected to find one of the rocky mesas rising here and there high above the jungle. "Up there," Tomisenkov pointed out to Alicharin, "the trees are standing farther apart. We can see the lights of the helicopters and hide till they give up the search."

Half an hour later they reached the rim of the plateau. Tomisenkov's guess had been correct. As far as they could see in the darkness the vegetation was much sparser but, on the other hand, dense enough so that the rocky surface could be seen from the helicopters only at a few places. Tomisenkov walked around these spots and looked for a location where he and his men could watch the searching aircraft.

They found the right spot. It was close behind the edge of the plateau. Toward the northwest a wall fell almost vertically down to the jungle. Behind the ridge lay a glen with a nearly flat bottom, well suited for a camping ground. Tomisenkov told Zelinskij, Breshnjew, Wlassow and Thora to take a rest while he and Alicharin stayed together on the rocky ledge and kept a watchful eye on the colorful lights of the helicopters.

Major Pjatkow—the man who had located Perry Rhodan's life raft and had dropped the bomb before the cave of the seals—had his radioman connect him with Colonel Raskujan. Pjatkow was one of Raskujan's favorite officers, so the connection was made without delay.

"I've got an idea," Pjatkow began without further introduction. "The search area is quite uniform—completely level up to the southern precipice of the mountain. But Tomisenkov couldn't have gone that far. There's only one other outstanding feature of the landscape, a vast mesa rising about 100 to 120 feet above the jungle. Tomisenkov needs a place from which he can observe our mission to see how close we get or when we'll break off our pursuit. He knows that we're forced to fly with our lights on. All he has to do is find a convenient lookout and watch us leisurely."

Raskujan wasn't quite convinced. "In which direction is this mesa located?" he asked.

"Southeast of the shot-down gunship."

"We figure it's Tomisenkov's intention to get to

the defense screen of the fortress which is northeast."

Pjatkow was ready with an answer. "I believe," he said, "Tomisenkov has thought along the same line. After we discovered a point on his route of escape, he realized his goal was known to us. Tomisenkov will march in any direction except where we're looking for him until we abandon our effort."

"H'm," Raskujan mumbled.

"I suggest," Pjatkow continued eagerly, "we secretly land two or three 'copters on that bluff and surprise Tomisenkov in his hideaway. If all other machines raise enough hell it won't be difficult for us to set down on the plateau unobtrusively."

Raskujan finally consented. Pjatkow ended his conversation and instructed two other machines of his formation to follow him. They flew away northeast almost as far as the cliffs of the mountain, switched off their lights when they reached a point where they were sure they could no longer be seen from the plateau, then returned and approached the elevated plain from the eastern direction.

The aircraft touched down in a little clearing not far from the rim and the men climbed out. Pjatkow held them back for a few minutes to make sure that nothing suspicious or dangerous lurked in the shadows. Then he gave the order to move.

The men didn't particularly care for the task at hand. They had never left their camp except in helicopters or in relatively safe rubber boats but after marching for 20 minutes their fear of the unknown was beginning to diminish.

Pjatkow estimated the length of the way to be

traversed to the opposite rim as about three miles. He figured this distance could be covered, even in the darkness, in about one and a half to two hours.

Then he'd show Raskujan that he was right!

Alicharin turned around.

"What's the matter?" Tomisenkov grunted.

A moment later Alicharin answered: "I believe I heard something ... from over there!" He pointed across the mesa.

"Nonsense!" Tomisenkov muttered. "What did you hear?"

"A helicopter!"

"Do you still hear it?"

"Not now!"

"Well, well," Tomisenkov said, leaning again on his elbows. "How would they get in back of us? They're all out there in front."

Alicharin thought that the argument was rather foolish. Nothing was easier for a helicopter than to fly around the plateau and land on the opposite side. But as long as he was uncertain whether he'd heard right, he preferred to say nothing.

He was startled when machineguns suddenly began to chatter over the jungle. Tomisenkov raised himself up a little more and stared with amazed eyes into the dark night. Then he began to laugh. "Wonderful!" he exclaimed. "One of these idiots thinks he's found us."

The shooting didn't last very long. Without apparent reason it stopped just as quickly as it had started. Simultaneously the battery of lights began to move around irregularly. The helicopters broke off the search and veered away. Minutes later they were out of sight. Only the whistling of the jets could be heard for a time.

"I don't understand it," Tomisenkov commented. He remained still for awhile and then got up. "Are you tired?" he asked Alicharin.

"No, chief."

"Alright. I'll lie down a little. Keep your eyes open. I'll tell Breshnjew to relieve you in one hour."

Major Pjatkow carried very powerful night-binoculars which were equipped with a small infra-red searchlight and filter.

With these binoculars he detected the campground in the dell close behind the eastern rim of the plateau. He posted his men in a circle around the camp and instructed them to overpower and seize the sleepers at his command.

Taking a second look, he then noticed one of the fugitives was absent. Six had been reported missing together with the Arkonide woman—among them Wlassow who, as was taken for granted, had made common cause with Tomisenkov.

Yet Pjatkow counted only five sleeping figures. One was gone.

Where was he?

Pjatkow took the chance of weakening his small troop of soldiers by sending one of his men to track down the sixth fugitive.

Then he waited.

Breshnjew had not yet shown up. He probably was

still sleeping. Alicharin didn't mind. He wasn't tired and he liked gazing into the dark although there was nothing to see.

There was a faint rustling. It came up the wall, slithering and scraping. Now it sounded right below and behind. Alicharin crawled five feet over to the side and noticed that the noise was still vertically below him.

He uttered a curse and ran fifteen feet farther. The noise was there, too. He had to move another 30 feet away before he left the rustling and scraping down there behind him.

He kneeled down and waited. Something seemed to move in the darkness but he was unable to see what it was.

Then a dark shiny object appeared over the edge of the rock. The movement Alicharin had seen came from two shapes looking like feelers attached to the black substance.

Alicharin jumped up.

Ants!

He was considerably relieved to notice that the insects didn't move in the direction of the camp. They crawled in a wide swath over the rocky ledge and moved rustling and crackling through the bushes— each one as long as two hands of a grown man!

Nevertheless, Alicharin walked to the campground. Venusian ants were unpredictable insects. Besides, nobody knew whether they had a sense of smell that would enable them to locate human prey.

Tomisenkov must be warned.

"There—!"

Alicharin hit the ground instantaneously and noiselessly when a shadow loomed out of the darkness in front of him. For one second he felt like a fool because of his timid reaction. It probably was Breshnjew coming to relieve him.

Yet it couldn't be Breshnjew!

Or anyone of Tomisenkov's team. The man was very tall, over six feet. Alicharin could clearly see his silhouette from below against the gray sky.

The stranger passed Alicharin only six feet away, moving cautiously and constantly turning his head. He hadn't discovered the ants yet but the neighborhood gave him the creeps anyhow.

Alicharin's thoughts were in a dither. He remembered the helicopters he'd heard more than an hour ago.

Perhaps he'd been right after all?

He followed the man crawling behind him. To his right—less than five feet away—was the army of ants.

The tall man stopped at the rim of the rock. He looked right and left and suddenly discovered the ants. Alicharin saw him raise his submachinegun in horror and spread his legs to gain a secure stance.

At this moment Alicharin jumped him.

The man, scared to death by the ants, offered no resistance. Alicharin kicked him behind the knee and hit the back of his neck with the edge of his hand.

The man toppled forward screaming in panic. He tumbled into the midst of the ants. He flailed around to defend himself against the insects inundating him. His submachinegun was flung in a wide curve over the rim of the bluff.

Alicharin crawled back and hid for a short time in the bushes. Then he darted forward again. The campground was in danger! The man, who had been assailed by the ants and killed in the meantime, hadn't come alone.

But Alicharin had taken less than ten steps when he noticed that he was already too late to bring help. He saw shadowy figures moving swiftly in the campground. He could hear muffled shouts. Somebody cursed—it was Zelinskij's voice.

Too late!

Alicharin whipped around and tried to get away from the scene of the raid as quickly as possible.

Chapter Five

CLIMAX ON VENUS

Nothing could be found at the place where the shooting fray must have occurred. By now they were about 600 feet above the level of the coastal plain. They had no way of knowing that the shooting was merely a decoy for Pjatkow's secret landing on the plateau.

Rhodan had monitored for awhile the intercommunications of the helicopters with his wristband radio. They revealed clearly that Raskujan's fliers were on a hunt for escaped prisoners. Rhodan assumed that some of Tomisenkov's followers had broken out. He didn't learn that Thora had managed to gain her freedom. The reports mentioned only "fugitives."

In the meantime Rhodan and his companions were only a few more miles away from the periphery of the barrier. Rhodan decided to take a rest for an hour before tackling the last stretch.

Raskujan was filled with pride and triumph. His two most important prisoners were hauled before him in the command center of his flagship. He looked at them with a cynical smile and asked: "What did you expect to accomplish with your escapade?"

Tomisenkov had not yet had a chance to clean up and to improve his battered appearance. His hair was mussed up and his old ragged uniform had been torn in the hand-to-hand fighting with Pjatkow's soldiers.

Thora had not taken part in the brief fracas. Soiled, but unbowed, she stood before Raskujan.

Neither Tomisenkov nor Thora answered the colonel.

"Aha!" Raskujan snickered. "Still as proud as ever!" He sat down comfortably and folded his legs. "I regret your stubbornness," he continued. "You're opposing the only real power on Venus. Why?"

Thora smiled scornfully. Tomisenkov snorted, "Because we can't stand you."

Raskujan didn't let this irritate him. "I've a more businesslike attitude," he gently chided Tomisenkov. "The three of us ought to be united. I'm convinced that together we can establish a superpower such as the world has never seen before."

Tomisenkov grinned contemptuously. "This presupposes the condition that Rhodan won't bother you."

"Oh!" Raskujan gestured. "He's left me alone for a whole year and why shouldn't he leave me alone in the future? Besides," he nodded to Thora, "if I can enter the fortress with your support, it'll be impossible for Rhodan to land on Venus against my will."

"Don't count on my help to get you into the base," Thora shouted angrily.

"I've got ways to make you do it," Raskujan threatened, beginning to lose his composure.

Thora made a disdainful gesture. "Who are you to force an Arkonide to do anything? Besides, you'll be in Rhodan's hands before you're through talking."

Raskujan jumped to his feet. "Rhodan isn't even here on Venus!" he shouted uncontrollably. "And if he tries to land here, I'll know how to keep him away."

At this point Thora's emotions got the better of her. With fire in her eyes she exclaimed: "You won't have to worry about preventing Rhodan's landing on Venus. He's already here!"

She realized she had made a mistake the moment the words slipped out. But to see Raskujan turn pale and stagger back to his chair was worth making a mistake.

Behind her she could hear Tomisenkov say softly: "You shouldn't have given him a warning!"

Alicharin kept marching. With the patience of an Asian he tried against all obstacles to reach a goal the existence of which he could so far only guess.

While being held in Raskujan's prison camp, he had heard about the weird events occurring over the open sea—the light that had been observed and that two helicopters had failed to return, as well as about Major Pjatkow's extensive search, the discovery of an empty lifeboat and the dropping of an atomic bomb.

Alicharin knew more than that. He remembered the ambush on the strip of land near Tomisenkov's camp a few days before Raskujan attacked the post. The ambush had been repulsed. Three men had been sighted but none captured.

Alicharin also remembered well the impulse-beamers used by the New Power during the fighting a year ago. The bursts of light over the ocean described by Raskujan's men probably originated from such weapons.

The rest was nothing but speculation and guesswork. If three members of the New Power were stranded on Venus, apparently virtually deprived of technical aids, Alicharin figured that their most urgent goal would be to get in touch with the positronic brain inside the fortress.

These were the reasons that Alicharin marched toward the mountains. He was aware that the huge protection field had a diameter of 30 miles, representing a periphery of about 95 miles. He realized that the odds for meeting the three men somewhere in these 95 miles were pitifully small; but they were improved by the fact that they—just like Alicharin—were approaching from the south and would probably try to enter the barrier from that direction.

However small his hope to find them was, it was the only chance he had. Wherever else he turned, the outlook was much bleaker than linking up with the citizens of the New Power.

Therefore he continued marching in the chosen direction.

When he had climbed halfway up the mountains he perceived at last the shimmering dome of the protective screen between two peaks touching the ceiling of clouds above.

By this time the vegetation had become less profuse and the going was much easier.

Alicharin's spirit was buoyed up and he walked very briskly.

No matter what people thought of Raskujan, they had to admit that sometimes he was capable of analyzing the situation.

From the onset he'd been puzzled by Major Pjatkow's report concerning the three men. Who would dare to cross the Venusian ocean at night in a puny boat, though it was only a 200 mile wide channel?

Raskujan knew that there was a possibility, no matter how small, that the three men had survived the cannon fire and the bomb.

What if one of these three people was Perry Rhodan?

Raskujan followed his train of thought and came to the same conclusion as Alicharin at about the same time although at a different place.

If Rhodan had ventured out to sea in the liferaft, it meant that, for some reason, he must have lost contact with Earth as well as with the Venusian bulwark. Otherwise he would have been in possession of far more technical equipment than seemed to be at his disposal at this time.

With this view in mind it was a fairly simple matter to conclude that Rhodan would do his utmost to reach the barrier and penetrate to the base. Raskujan didn't doubt for a minute that this was entirely in Rhodan's power to achieve.

The logical consequence of this deduction was an order to the entire fleet of helicopters to fly to the defense barrier and shoot at anything moving in the vicinity. However, Raskujan kept it a secret that this massive action was directed against Perry Rhodan. He was afraid that the mere mentioning of his name would put a terrible fear in his men.

After an interval that was unanimously considered far too short by all crews, the helicopters took off again.

Raskujan observed the start from the brightly lit helipad by television and felt some reassurance, seeing the spectacle of his gunships lifting off and racing away.

He didn't consider it in the least ironic that the greatest of all actions launched on Venus was intended for a single man. If he'd had more fighting strength available, he'd have deployed 10 times as many men and machines to seize and destroy this single man:

Perry Rhodan!

Rhodan's maltreated body had used the last period of rest to protest the constant neglect it had suffered: it reacted with an attack of fever. His teeth were chattering audibly when it was time to depart again. Marshall and the Japanese suggested that he wait until the fever passed but Rhodan answered with a grim laugh: "I'm afraid that this old ticker," he pointed to his chest, "is going to act up as long as I don't give it something better to do."

They continued on their trek. They were fortunate that the diminishing vegetation hampered their progress less and less.

Rhodan, however, was plagued by bad luck. He was forced to revise his opinion about his ticker. His attack of fever didn't let up, it was growing stronger and stronger. At times he had to hold onto Marshall to keep from falling down.

Shortly after 229:00 o'clock they traversed a small valley high in the mountains and, passing through its exit, were regaled with the magnificent sight of the gleaming dome over the base, seemingly close enough to touch.

Rhodan breathed a sigh of relief. They had almost accomplished their task, a task that had required superhuman efforts.

The terrain they were crossing now was a high rocky plain with a few bushes far and between. They made good time and the glistening wall of the barrier moved perceptibly closer.

"Only twenty-five hundred feet to go," Marshall murmured after awhile to encourage Rhodan and to take his mind off his pains. He scarcely had finished his sentence when a light buzz arose from south of the mountains. Marshall hesitated and Rhodan, who was leaning on his shoulder, also stood still.

Son Okura spun around and stared at the dark sky.

The humming grew louder and reverberated over the high valley they had just passed through and dissolved in the whistling of jets and whirring of rotor blades.

"Choppers!" shouted the Japanese. "At least 40 of them!"

With an abrupt and determined effort Rhodan stood up under his own power. He looked hurriedly around. "Take cover!" he panted. "Over there! Try to reach the side of the valley!"

For a few minutes Alicharin had the impression that the huge fleet was sent to track him down. He watched the whirlybirds zooming over him where he had quickly concealed himself and as they began to circle around the shimmering energy curtain.

93

Alicharin soon understood what they were after. Someone had come to the same conclusion as he and were attempting to capture the three men from the New Power where they were most likely to be found.

Without further delay he set out again and after a short time came to a tortuous pass crossing over the last mountain chain separating him from his destination and leading beyond at the western end into a high vale surrounded by steep walls.

Farther north—perhaps a little more than a mile— the shining dome rose from the floor of the valley.

However, the helicopters were also circling up north as Alicharin could hear distinctly. Being familiar with the efficiency of their infra-red searchlight, he kept strictly under cover. This slowed him down quite a bit but he advanced with safety.

The helicopters scoured the valley at low altitude. Rhodan and his companions had been unable to reach the wall of the gorge and sought cover in the shadow of a huge boulder. When they saw that they had not yet been detected, they retreated farther and took refuge in a shallow cave indented in the steep western wall of the ravine. From there Son Okura observed the gunships. "They're dividing up," he said. "Two formations are flying east and west along the defense shield and the third's cruising in front of the shield."

Rhodan could barely muster enough strength for an answer. "We've got to go on," he whispered. "We can contact the positronic brain only at the border of the field."

Marshall remonstrated. "In your place I'd rather ..."

"Uh uh!" Rhodan silenced him, pushing himself up on the wall of the cave.

At the same moment Son Okura, who was standing at the entrance of the cave whirled around with a muffled shout and raised his thermo-gun. "Halt!"

A barely audible voice came from the dark shadows to the right of the cave. Marshall couldn't understand a word. He left Rhodan alone and went to the side of the Japanese with his weapon ready to fire. "Who's there?" he demanded.

Okura shrugged his shoulders. "He claims to be one of Tomisenkov's men and that he ran away from the prison camp."

Marshall lowered his gun. He closed his eyes while Okura kept the stranger covered with his impulse-beamer and concentrated on the thoughts flowing from the brain of the unknown man. "He's OK," he finally nodded to Okura. "The man has no hostile intentions."

Okura lowered his weapon as well. He called to the stranger to come closer.

Then Marshall saw him emerge from the darkness. He was fairly small but very broad-shouldered, with small slanted eyes and high cheekbones. He turned to Son Okura and said: "My name is Alicharin and I'm a member of General Tomisenkov's forces. I've got some important information to give you."

Although he had no time to lose, Rhodan was anxious to hear his report. Alicharin quickly recounted the details of the events since Raskujan's raid on Tomisenkov's post.

"After what happened it won't be easy for Thora to resist Raskujan," Rhodan murmured. "He'll do anything to make her talk. We really must hurry!"

They left the cave and proceeded along the wall. Taking advantage of any cover they could find, they sneaked forward while Son Okura continously kept a sharp eye on the helicopters. Alicharin's report and his fear about Thora's fate seemed to have given Perry Rhodan a second wind. He was able to walk half the remaining distance on his own legs until he was forced to lean on Marshall again.

They approached the luminous wall within 50 feet without having been spotted by Raskujan's machines. But from here on it became crucial.

The last stretch of territory was virtually devoid of a place to hide. There were only a few isolated rocks, scarcely big enough to give protection for one man.

Rhodan anticipated that their foes would drop bombs as soon as they had spied their victims and those little rocks provided no protection whatsoever against bombs.

It was plain to see that Rhodan had reached the limit of his strength. His cheeks were sunken and red splotches dotted his skin. His voice was hoarse and he wheezed with every effort. "We've got to create a diversionary maneuver," he instructed his friends. "One of us will have to draw their attention away from the others. While they're kept busy by him, the rest of us will rush to the barrier. I expect that the positronic brain will only require a few seconds to identify me and to open the barrier for a moment. Who wants to volunteer?"

"I'll go," Alicharin said at once.

Rhodan had no objection, at least none for which he could take time to bring up. Alicharin was not a citizen of the New Power; it was not his duty to risk his life in a bold maneuver. However, there was no time for a debate.

Alicharin sneaked away after it was pointed out to him that he would have to start running like the very devil as soon as the defense screen was dimmed. Nobody knew what he planned to do to distract the gunships.

They waited—feverishly and impatiently.

In Major Pjatkow's opinion the high valley leading from the south to the energy dome was the most plausible place where the fugitives could be intercepted.

Pjatkow didn't have the slightest notion whom he was hunting but he assumed that either a lot of people were involved or that they were especially dangerous as Raskujan made such extraordinary efforts to catch them.

He looked at his watch. They had only enough fuel for five hours flight. Then they'd have to return for refuelling. Within five hours the unknown persons had to ...

"There!" the observer exclaimed. "A man!"

Pjatkow pushed the observer to the side and peered through the filter eyepiece. There was a man moving between the rocks below. He was only 60 feet away from the barrier and was running like mad.

"Fire!" Pjatkow barked.

The observer squeezed himself behind the automatic cannon, aimed at the moving target and began to shoot. He was disgusted to see his projectiles explode far from the runner and corrected his aim but before he managed to focus on the target, the man had disappeared behind a boulder.

Major Pjatkow was breathing excitedly. "Lower! Lower!"

The aircraft descended.

"Circle around the rock!"

The pilot banked the aircraft and began to fly in a wide circle. "Closer!" Pjatkow shouted angrily. And then he discerned another movement from the corner of his eye. He pulled his viewer around and detected three men one hundred feet away scurrying to the radiant barrier. He instantly grasped that the man below him had only executed a feint.

The real danger was that group of men over there!

"To the left!" he yelled at the pilot. "We've got to get them first!"

The flier, who saw only the events straight ahead of him, wasted little time responding to the command and changed his course.

"Faster!" Pjatkow urged. "Get the bombs ready!" He slammed down the switch of the radio transmitter at his side with a crack. It was unnecessary to waste words to explain his actions. The other machines were able to determine from his orders what was afoot.

The fleeing men reached the barrier.

"Bombs ready!" the observer reported.

Pjatkow took notice that two other machines were flying beside him and were laying down heavy fire from their automatic cannons.

The bombs the observer was about to unleash were ordinary high-explosive shells. It wasn't feasible for a helicopter flying at low altitudes to drop a nuclear bomb no matter how small.

However, the high-explosive bombs were more than adequate to ...

The radiant dome was gone!

Pjatkow uttered a piercing scream of horror as the barrier vanished. Yet at the same instance he grasped the unique chance that suddenly was offered to him. "To the right!" he bellowed to the pilot. "Get through the barrier!"

The pilot didn't measure up to the task. He fumbled around for five seconds before he changed his course. Pjatkow was fuming.

At last the machine turned around and raced with top speed toward the place where only moments before the protective shield had towered above the floor of the valley.

Nobody in Pjatkow's helicopter got even a glimpse when the barrier began to radiate again at the precise instant that the machine was about to push through to the field inside.

A brilliant explosion was all the other helicopters could see as their radios crackled sharply. A shower of flaming debris fell to the ground and was soon extinguished.

It was impossible for anyone to say later whether Pjatkow's gunship had been swallowed up by the energy of the reactivated defense screen or had been torn apart by its own bombs exploding under the impact.

Following the initial shock of terror the accompanying helicopter crews recognized that everything had been restored in the aftermath to the previous state after the short interruption and that the unknown people had obviously succeeded in setting foot inside the defense field during the few seconds the barrier had been lifted.

Colonel Raskujan received the terse communique: "Major Pjatkow killed in action. Unable to apprehend fugitives. Escaped into fortress."

Raskujan was fully aware of the significance of the message that Rhodan had reached the safety of the fortress.

He assumed that it would be merely a matter of minutes before Rhodan would attack his post with the superior technical means at his command and completely wipe them out.

He ordered the defense alert for his post which required no extensive preparations or changes. Since the day he landed his replacement fleet on Venus he had anticipated such contingencies and deployed his troops and equipment in such a manner that they could defend themselves in all directions.

It was a different question, however, whether the strategic placement of his troops would have any effect against the technical juggernaut to be expected from Perry Rhodan.

As Raskujan was of the opinion that this question had to be answered in the negative, he took another step to prepare for this turn of events, keeping it a secret from everybody except the pilot he needed to fly his helicopter.

Together with the pilot Raskujan tied up the hands of his two most prominent prisoners, Thora and Tomisenkov, behind their backs. At gunpoint he drove the couple to the waiting aircraft and helped them to climb in.

As Tomisenkov was shoved into the gunship by the hard fists of the pilot, he looked back over his shoulder and said derisively: "Something went wrong, didn't it? The rats are leaving the sinking ship!"

"Shut up!" Raskujan growled, saying no more.

The cockpit was roomier than in other helicopters. There were four passenger seats. Thora and Tomisenkov were put in the first two while Raskujan sat behind them with his cocked gun. The pilot squeezed into his narrow seat and waited for something. The doors clicked shut.

"Listen to me!" Raskujan began with a strained voice. "My overriding concern now is not to fall into the hands of Perry Rhodan. Rhodan has managed to get into the base and he's bound to arrive here in a few minutes. My situation is very desperate.

"I'm taking you both with me. You, Tomisenkov, because you know your way around on Venus and you, Thora, as hostage for Rhodan.

"It'll be your job, Tomisenkov, to find a safe hideout for us where we can stay till Rhodan is ready to negotiate with me.

"My situation is so critical you can rest assured I'd kill you before I'd let you ruin my last chance.

"Tomisenkov, give the pilot instructions where to fly!"

"Fly between 270 and 280°!" he grudgingly told the pilot. "Climb up to an altitude of 1500 feet because we'll soon get to the mountains."

Perry Rhodan had enough strength left to formulate a message for the positronic brain which was transmitted telepathically by Marshall. It was a fair assumption that the brain, once its attention had been drawn to Rhodan, would correctly interpret the message and act accordingly.

The instructions included a request for a vehicle enabling them to travel as quickly as possible to the center of the base and for medication to restore Rhodan's freedom of action without delay.

Alicharin had not only survived the bombardment from Pjatkow's helicopter without getting hurt but had also managed to dart at the right moment into the field of the base.

Rhodan finally lost consciousness as soon as he had given his instructions to Marshall. The telepath kept repeating his message until Son Okura saw a glider approach with high speed close above the ground. They carried Rhodan inside and took their seats. A few minutes later the glider was admitted through the portal of the mountain fortress and Rhodan was led to a room where the medicine was administered.

In half an hour Rhodan had recuperated enough to be in a position to issue his commands. He instructed the positronic brain to lift the barrier girdling the entire planet so that Reginald Bell could at last land in his auxiliary spaceship: In order not to complicate matters, he further requested that the regular protective border surrounding the base in normal times at a diameter of 300 miles shouldn't be reinstated in place of the special mantle shrouding the planet during the emergency.

Finally Reginald Bell was commissioned to finish the current military action on Rhodan's behalf and was given the necessary detailed information.

Only then, after having attended to the final measures, did Rhodan conclude that the time had come for him and his exhausted friends to relax from their super-human efforts. They fell into a long sleep.

Bell reacted with the raging energy of a pent-up volcano whose fiery eruption had been barred by a crust of earth.

The *Guppy*—one of the auxiliary spaceships measuring 200 feet in diameter—swooped down with activated shock screens full speed ahead into the lower strata of the Venusian atmosphere. At Mach 15—fifteen times the velocity of sound—the air molecules around the shock screen became ionized and began to light up. With a brilliant blue-white trail of ionized air the ship shot through the Venusian night like a gigantic comet in all its splendor. It appeared over Raskujan's camp spreading stark terror among the defenders who had never before seen such an awesome spectacle.

Nobody dared shoot at the vessel. It was totally impervious to missiles made on Earth in any case. Coming to a stop at about 300 feet above the encampment, it hovered motionlessly above the ground. Bell took no chances. He ordered Tako Kakuta, the teleporter, to use the psycho-beamer to saturate the entire territory with hypnotic commands for surrender.

Afterwards the spaceship touched down and Bell began to take stock. He knew that Thora was held prisoner in this camp and despite his ambivalent feelings toward her, her well-being was foremost in his mind.

He was unable to find her. His newly-made captives were quite willing to show him the part of the camp where Thora had been detained since they were under the influence of the hypnotic spell. However, she was missing and nobody seemed to know where she could be.

After awhile it was also noted that General Tomisenkov was among the missing and when it became known that Raskujan had fled too, Bell began to get the picture emerging from the facts of the case.

At the same time he realized that it was useless to track down the culprit. Raskujan was sure to come forward as soon as the situation was cleared up and as long as Thora was at his mercy there was very little that could be done to bring him to his knees.

"Between the two mountain peaks!" Tomisenkov directed the flier.

The pilot gave him a running report of his findings on the observation instrument and Tomisenkov advised him accordingly as to his course.

In Tomisenkov's estimation they had put about 90 miles between themselves and the army post in the last two hours. They were slowed down by the numerous peaks and the complicated way of communicating flying instructions.

Their speed was further reduced by Tomisenkov's endeavor to gain time. He waited for Raskujan to relax his vigilance and hoped that Thora would create some commotion to divert his attention.

"There are several other peaks behind them," the pilot stated. "Three in a row. The one in the middle is about two and a half to three thousand feet high."

"Keep between the center and the left peak and then set your course at 265°."

Raskujan cleared his throat. "Are you sure you know where you're going?"

"Of course," Tomisenkov snorted.

At this moment Thora uttered a shrill scream and clung close to Tomisenkov.

"What's the matter?" Raskujan asked gruffly.

Thora shuddered. "There!" she cried, frightened. "A flying reptile!"

She stared out the window at the side as if she were seeing something out there. Her horror was so well pretended that Tomisenkov didn't know at first whether or not a lizard was actually flying by.

Raskujan slid over to the next seat and pressed his face against the plexiglass. His automatic pistol was lying across his knees.

Tomisenkov spun abruptly around. He got up on his seat with his knees and bent forward. Before Raskujan was aware what was going on, Tomisenkov pushed his back against him and pinned him down. He raised his hands behind him in his doubled up position and gripped Raskujan by the throat. He choked the colonel with brute force but was unable to see what effect he had on him.

"Stop it!" Thora shouted. "You're strangling him."

Meanwhile the pilot was aroused. He turned his head and looked back.

"Watch the chopper or we'll smash up!" Tomisenkov yelled at him.

Raskujan fell limp in his seat when Tomisenkov released his grip and moved away. With his hands still tied, he picked up the automatic pistol and propped it up between two seats, pointing it at the pilot. Then he told him: "You better believe me, I can pull the trigger with my hands tied behind my back and without looking. One false move and you're dead. Now turn around and fly back to the camp!"

It was an incredible situation. Tomisenkov kneeled on the seat where a moment ago Raskujan had been sitting. He was facing the back of the seat and held the trigger of the gun behind him between the two forward seats. Although he would have no trouble shooting the weapon, it would be the end of him if it slipped off the target.

Fortunately it was a simple matter to free his hands from the ropes now that Raskujan was immobilized. Thora pulled out a little pocket knife he had managed to conceal in his pants and cut his bonds.

From then on, everything was child's play. The pilot had never been especially enamored of Raskujan as a beloved commander. His orders had not impressed him as very sensible and all he needed was the little reminder of the gun pointed at him to obey

Tomisenkov unconditionally, willingly and promptly.

Tomisenkov turned to Raskujan with the intention of taking care of him. He was profoundly shocked when he found that the colonel was dead.

He covered him with his jacket.

"He deserved it," the general commented, "but I feel sorry for him just the same."

A few hours past midnight Rhodan's arrival was announced. Using a craft from the base, Rhodan set down in Raskujan's former post close to Reginald Bell's auxiliary ship. The camp was lit brightly.

Rhodan had been briefed on the news that had transpired in the meantime. He knew that Raskujan had tried to abduct Thora and Tomisenkov and that both ex-prisoners had returned to the camp with Raskujan's body.

After entering the command center of the auxiliary ship, Bell gave him a formal report. He passed on a request by Tomisenkov: "The general respectfully asks for an audience."

Rhodan nodded. "Where's Thora?"

Bell shrugged his shoulders. "I gather she wants to be alone. I always let her do what she wants."

Rhodan nodded a second time. "Well, then let Tomisenkov come in!"

Bell left the command center and Tomisenkov soon appeared in the door. Rhodan offered him a chair.

"You'll be surprised," Tomisenkov began without preamble, "what I'm going to propose to you."

Rhodan was amused by his direct approach. "Go ahead."

"I've already talked to Raskujan's men before your arrival," the general said. "I described to them how we've lived on Venus for a whole year with a minimum of technical support and how comfortable we would have been if we'd been blessed with the benefits of modern technology. I've submitted a proposal that we remain on Venus in the future ... and they've agreed! All except four or five."

He looked hopefully at Rhodan.

"Excellent!" Rhodan replied. "I've no objections to your settling down on Venus as long as you don't interfere with the fortress."

Tomisenkov shook his head. "That's the farthest thing from our minds. We've all learned in the meantime what's happened to the government of the Eastern Bloc. My people and myself have written off the past long ago and it was apparently not very difficult for Raskujan's men to do the same."

Rhodan got up and paced the floor. Suddenly Tomisenkov heard him laugh. "I didn't think my plans would come true so quickly," Rhodan exclaimed.

"Your plans?" Tomisenkov expressed astonishment

"Yes, my plans! Why do you think I chose not to obliterate you and your entire fleet a year ago?"

"I don't know—why?" Tomisenkov stuttered.

"Because I believed," Rhodan explained to him, "that if I let your people live, you would develop into a healthy stock for the first colony of Venus. It was an experiment with humans and you've stood the test."

Tomisenkov was so amazed that his mouth gaped

open. Only slowly did it dawn on him that he had acted during these last months like a puppet on a string. His mind resisted acceptance of this knowledge and when it finally had sunk in, anger welled up in him.

But only for a second.

It was no shame to be pulled on invisible strings by a man like Perry Rhodan!

Rhodan seemed able to read his thoughts.

"You needn't feel that your pride has been hurt," he said calmly. "I merely conceived an idea. You had complete freedom of action and I don't mind saying that you handled yourself with great distinction.

"I've complete faith in you and I don't believe I'll go wrong if I leave you a free hand in establishing a new colony. I promise you my help."

As if in a dream Tomisenkov got up, walked toward Rhodan and shook his hand. "Thank you!" he murmured. "Thank you very much!"

As he left the room he was muttering excitedly to himself. Rhodan couldn't hear what he said.

Ten hours passed before Rhodan met the woman from Arkon again.

He'd paid no visit to her as yet. He remained in the command center taking care of dispositions prior to his return to Earth.

Thora eventually decided to go and see him.

The hatch slid open almost silently and she stood quietly for awhile in the opening before Rhodan noticed her. He recognized at a glance that she felt embarrassed and unsure of herself. How she must have been torn by her emotions! By her ill-considered flight from Terra she'd brought on a succession of unforseen disasters in which Rhodan had almost perished and the New Power brought close to downfall.

Falteringly she came closer. Perry got up, walked toward her. Confronting her, he took her hand between his.

Thora parted her pale lips to speak but Perry spoke first. "You'll never know," he said softly, intensely, "how happy I am to see you again."

His affectionate declaration completely shattered the composure of the queenly creature. She was unable to voice at all the apologies she had intended to offer, the explanation she had intended to give for her motivations. Instead she reacted with an astonishing gesture: she leaned forward till her silvery-white head touched Rhodan's shoulder—

And cried!

Thora, the proud Arkonide, with a heart encased in ice—cried!

Rhodan tried to console her. He made a few feeble attempts to comfort her but could think of nothing that didn't seem inadequate under the circumstances. So he simply stood still, a pillar of silent strength, and put his arms around Thora's shoulders, drawing her to him and letting her give full vent to her flood of tears.

"Crew's aboard!" Bell reported. "Ship ready for lift-off."

Rhodan directed his gaze to the observation screen. The first light of the new day on Venus shone on the horizon. "Time to go home," he said, lost in thought.

Bell reacted cheerfully. "Freyt's hair must have turned gray in the meantime. He knows next to nothing about our adventures on Venus, only such little scraps of information as I could give him."

Rhodan put the ship's telecom mike to his lips. "Lift-off in 60 seconds," he announced quietly.

Reginald Bell went to his post.

"Control check!"

Several levers clicked in place.

"No malfunctions!" Bell reported.

"All set. Blast off!"

The spaceship roared louder than a din of dinosaurs. Soon it was airborne in the ash-gray sky, destined to fly higher than any pterodactyl! Raskujan's camp—now controlled by Tomisenkov—was left far behind. To the northeast they caught a glimpse of the shimmering barrier surrounding the fortress.

With the advice and consent of the robot brain itself, the positronicomputer had been reprogrammed by Rhodan so that such undesirous actions as had happened in the past would never be repeated.

As the sun rose over the horizon, a big yellow lantern veiled by the clouded atmosphere, Rhodan mused pensively, "If it had always shone for us, we would have been spared many perils on Venus."

The Peacelord was headed home. But for how long could he hope to stay? Where might he be needed next?

Anywhere from Mars to the Milky Way.

In this solar system or among the stars.